A FOOL AND HIS HONEY

An Aurora Teagarden Mystery

BOOKS BY CHARLAINE HARRIS

Gunnie Rose

An Easy Death

A Longer Fall

Midnight, Texas

Midnight Crossroad

Day Shift

Night Shift

Sookie Stackhouse

Dead Until Dark

Living Dead in Dallas

Club Dead

Dead to the World

Dead as a Doornail

Definitely Dead

All Together Dead

From Dead to Worse

Dead and Gone

Dead in the Family

Dead Reckoning

Deadlocked

Dead Ever After

A Touch of Dead: The Sookie Stackhouse Companion

After Dead: What Came Next in the World of Sookie Stackhouse

Dead But Not Forgotten *‡

The Aurora Teagarden Mysteries

Real Murders †

A Bone to Pick †

Three Bedrooms, One Corpse †

The Julius House †

Dead Over Heels †

A Fool and His Honey †

Last Scene Alive

Poppy Done to Death †

All the Little Liars

Sleep Like a Baby

The Harper Connelly Mysteries

Grave Sight

Grave Surprise

An Ice Cold Grave

Grave Secret

Cemetery Girl
with Christopher Golden

The Pretenders

Inheritance

Haunted

The Lily Bard Mysteries

Shakespeare's Landlord

Shakespeare's Champion

Shakespeare's Christmas

Shakespeare's Trollop

Shakespeare's Counselor

Standalone Works

Small Kingdoms and Other Stories†

Sweet and Deadly †

A Secret Rage †

Dancers in the Dark †

Dancers in the Dark & Layla Steps Up †

Anthologies ‡

Many Bloody Returns

Wolfsbane and Mistletoe

Death's Excellent Vacation

Home Improvement: Undead Edition

An Apple for the Creature

Games Creatures Play

Weird World of Sports

* *anthology*

† *available as a JABberwocky edition*

‡ *co-edited with Toni L. P. Kelner*

A FOOL AND HIS HONEY

An Aurora Teagarden Mystery

CHARLAINE HARRIS

Published by JABberwocky Literary Agency, Inc.

A FOOL AND HIS HONEY

This paperback edition published in 2020 by
JABberwocky Literary Agency, Inc.

Cover design by Tiger Bright Studios

Paperback ISBN 978-1-625675-08-8

Ebook ISBN 978-1-625672-14-8

http://www.awfulagent.com/ebooks

For my family—
my mother, father, husband, and children—
who sustain me in all that I do.
Without you, it would hardly be worth doing.

ACKNOWLEDGMENTS

I thank the cybercitizens of DorothyL for their support, encouragement, and just being themselves, so that day by day I can "talk" to other people who love the mysterious world as much as I do. In the writing of this book, I particularly laud the Ohio contingent, who answered all my questions so patiently, and often at great trouble to themselves.

1

The day everything went rotten was the day the woodman went crazy in my backyard.

My mother and her husband, John Queensland, were just leaving when Darius Quattermain rattled up my driveway, his battered blue pickup pulling a trailer full of split oak. Mother (Aida Brattle Teagarden Queensland) had taken a moment from her busy day to bring me a dress she'd bought for me in Florida, where she'd been attending a convention for real estate brokers who'd sold over a million dollars worth of property in a year. John, who's retired, had come out with Mother just because he likes being with her.

As Darius was getting out of his truck, Mother was hugging me and saying, "John isn't feeling so well, Aurora, so we're going back to town." She always made it sound as though Martin and I lived on the frontier, instead of just a mile out of Lawrenceton. In fact, since there are fields all around our property, on clear days I could see the roof of her house, sitting on the edge of Lawrenceton's nicest suburb.

I looked at John, concerned, and saw that he did indeed look puny. John golfs, and normally he looks like a hale and hearty sixty-four-year-old. Actually, John's a handsome man ... and a good one. But at that moment he looked old and embarrassed, as men so often are by illness.

"You better go home and lie down," I said, concerned. "Call me if you need me, after Mother goes back to work?"

"Sure will, honey," John said heavily, and eased into the front passenger seat of Mother's Lincoln.

Mother gave my cheek a little brush with her lips, I thanked her again for the dress, and then while they maneuvered through turning around to head down our long driveway, I strolled over to Darius, who was pulling on heavy gloves.

I didn't suspect it, but a perfectly ordinary day—getting Martin off to work, going to my own job at the library, coming home with nothing more than a little housework planned—was about to go spectacularly wrong.

It began slowly.

"Where you want me to unload this wood, Miz Bartell?" Darius Quattermain asked.

"This area under the stairs, I think," I told him. We were standing by the garage, which is connected to the house by a covered walkway. On the side facing the house, there's a stairway going up to the little apartment over the garage.

"You not afraid of bugs getting into your siding there?" Darius asked dubiously.

I shrugged. "Martin picked the spot, and if he doesn't like it, he can move it."

Darius gave me a strange look, almost as if he'd never seen me before, which at the time I wrote off as conservative disapproval of my attitude toward my husband.

But he got down to work. After a brief conference, I'd given him the green light to pull the trailer as close as possible, and he began unloading rapidly in the chilly air. The sky was gray, and rain was supposed to start tonight. The wind began to pick up, blowing my long tangle of brown hair into my eyes. I shivered, and stuck my hands in the pockets of my heavy red sweater. As I turned to go inside, I looked over at the roses I'd planted at the corner of the concrete porch at the back of the house, outside my kitchen. They needed pruning, and I was trying to remember if I was supposed to do it now or wait until February, when a piece of wood flew by my head.

"Mr. Quattermain?" I said, whirling around. "You okay?"

Darius Quattermain, deacon of Antioch Holiness Church, began to sing "She'll Be Comin' Round the Mountain" in a manic bellow. He also kept up with his task, with one big difference. Instead of stacking the wood neatly under the stairs, Darius pitched split pieces of oak in all directions.

"Whoa!" I said loudly. Even to my own ears, I sounded panicky instead of authoritative. When the next piece of firewood missed my shoulder by only a foot or so, I retreated into the house, locking the door behind me. After a minute, I risked a peek out the window. Darius showed no signs of calming down, and there was still a lot of wood on the back of his pickup. I was thinking of it as ammunition now, instead of fuel.

I dialed the sheriff's department, since our house is outside the city limits.

"SPACOLEC," said Doris Post. "SPACOLEC" stands

for Sparling County Law Enforcement Complex. It sounded like Doris was chewing a mouthful of gum. I figured she must be trying to quit smoking again.

"Doris, this is Aurora Teagarden."

"Oh, hi, hon. How you doing?"

"Just fine, thank you, hope you're well. Ah—I have a situation here."

"Is that right? What's happening?"

"You know Darius Quattermain?"

"The black man who delivers wood? Got six kids? Wife works at Food Fantastic?"

"Right." I peered out the window, hoping that somehow the situation would have changed for the normal. Nope. "He's gone crazy."

"Whereabouts?"

"In my side yard. He seemed just fine when he got here, but all of a sudden he started singing and chunking wood."

"He's still there?"

"Yes, he is. As a matter of fact . . ." I stared out the window in appalled fascination. "Um, Doris, he's taking his clothes off now. And still singing. And chunking."

"You locked in that house, Roe?"

"Yes, and I've set the security system." Guiltily, I reached over and punched in the code. "I don't think he means to hurt anyone, Doris. He just can't help himself. It's like he took drugs, or had a seizure, or something. So whoever comes out here, if they could take it real easy?"

"I'll tell them what you said," Doris told me. She didn't sound bored or lackadaisical anymore. "You move away from the windows, Roe. A car's on the way."

"Thanks, Doris."

I hung up and hid behind a curtain, so I could check on Darius from time to time. I needn't have bothered to hide. I could have been on the surface of the moon for all Darius cared. He was one big brown goose pimple in the chilly breeze as he danced around buck naked, telling the sky that we would have the wedding supper when she came.

I wondered what Darius would do when he ran out of verses.

I didn't have to wait long. He switched to "Turkey in the Straw." Darius was having a flashback to elementary school music class, I decided.

He scampered around to his own music with an impressive light-footedness for a staid middle-aged man.

I decided to call my husband.

"There's a naked man in the backyard," I said softly, because Darius had stopped singing and was hunting an imaginary deer.

"Anyone I know?" Martin's voice was cautious. He wasn't certain how seriously to take this.

"Darius Quattermain. The woodman."

"I assume you've called the sheriff?"

"The car's here now." The official car had just pulled up my driveway. I nodded approvingly. The siren wasn't on and the lights stopped flashing as I watched. "Jimmy Henske and Levon Suit," I told Martin.

"Jimmy Henske, huh? Maybe I'd better come home." And the phone was replaced firmly in its cradle. Martin has no high opinion of the sheriff's department in Sparling County, and Jimmy Henske, who is maybe twenty-five, gawky and diffident, has never inspired my husband with his competence.

But Jimmy's a nice guy, and Levon Suit (who went to high school with me) is a very controlled deputy who is not only innately more intelligent than Jimmy but five years more experienced. I remembered that Levon had dated one of Darius's daughters when we were juniors.

I watched, fascinated, as Levon slowly approached Darius. I was a little surprised the deputy would brave walking right up to him—but then, it was completely obvious Darius wasn't carrying a weapon. It appeared that Darius had killed the deer and resumed singing and dancing in celebration. In fact, he was so glad to see Levon that he grabbed Levon's hands and capered off, and for a delirious minute or two Levon trotted right along with him.

With a patience that made me proud, the two deputies coaxed Darius into their car. Jimmy hurried back to pick up Darius's clothes, which he tossed in the front seat.

"Yessir, we'll sing along with you all the way into town," Jimmy was saying earnestly, as Martin parked beside the squad car. My husband emerged from the Mercedes looking, as he generally did, immaculate, prosperous, and handsome.

"Hey, Mr. Bartell!" Darius called happily, as Jimmy was shutting the car door. "I brought your wood!"

Martin stood on the covered sidewalk between our house and the garage and saw the pieces of oak scattered around the backyard, which we'd finally, expensively, had rolled and reseeded to make it smooth and grassy. Quite a few divots had been ripped out of the turf by Darius's impromptu log toss.

"Thanks a lot, Darius," Martin said.

I came out after the squad car had departed, all three of the occupants singing away. I mentally filed away a decision to write a letter to Sheriff Padgett Lanier to commend Levon and Jimmy's restraint and good sense.

Martin was shedding his suit coat and pulling on his own heavy gloves from the toolshed built into the back of the garage. He got the wheelbarrow, too.

Besides my heavy red cardigan, I was still wearing my work clothes, a long sleeveless denim dress over a red T-shirt, but Martin was setting such a good example that my inappropriate clothes were no excuse to be idle. I found my own gloves and helped out. As we worked, we speculated on this bizarre event and whether Darius, though clearly not in his right mind, had actually broken a law by dancing naked in our yard.

"How was the library this morning?" Martin asked, after we'd stacked the last piece of wood. I stood back, feeling sweat bead on my forehead from the exertion though the air was bracingly chilly, and smiled at him. He knew I was happier now that I'd resumed part-time work at the Lawrenceton library.

"Sam decided patrons with overdue books would be more likely to return the books if they were called personally, rather than sent a postcard. This comes from him reading some study in a magazine, of course. So guess who got to make at least fifty phone calls this morning? Thank God for answering machines. I decided it wasn't cheating to leave a message on the machine." I watched Martin pull off his heavy gloves. "What about you?"

"I had my annual physical, followed by a morning-long meeting about implementing the new EPA regulations."

My husband Martin, who has a pirate gene stuck somewhere in his DNA, frequently gets frustrated with his job as vice president of manufacturing for Pan-Am Agra, an agricultural products company. He has not always done something so legitimate and safe.

"Sorry, honey." I patted his shoulder sympathetically. We strolled back to return the things to our toolshed. Darius's pickup and small trailer were still parked blocking my car in, halfway on the gravel and halfway on the grass; when I'd okayed that, I'd only expected him to be there for a little while. The ground had been nice and dry, but as I turned to go back into the house, big drops of rain began to patter down. We simultaneously thought of the truck making troughs in the softened dirt, and hurried back to check the cab of the truck.

Martin said a heartfelt and obscene word. The ignition was empty.

I looked in the passenger side. Perhaps Darius had just withdrawn the keys and tossed them on the seat to silence the little beeper that reminds you your keys are in the ignition. I do that occasionally, if I have to run back into the house for a minute or two.

"Look, Martin." I pointed. But not at a set of keys.

Martin stuck his head in the door.

There was an open bottle of generic pain reliever, acetaminophen, on the seat.

Martin raised one eyebrow at me. "So?"

"He started acting so funny so fast, my first thought was that he'd taken a drug. And I don't think he's the kind of man who would ever think of doing something so dangerous."

Martin said, "We'd better call the sheriff's department again."

So once again Jimmy and Levon drove the mile out of town that got them to our house, and Jimmy pulled on plastic gloves before he picked up the pill bottle. He poured its contents onto the gloved palm of his other hand. He didn't tell us to leave, so we watched.

Martin saw it first. He pointed.

Levon bent over Jimmy's palm.

"Damn," he said in his deep voice.

One of the pills was a smidge smaller than the others, and not quite the same shade of white. It didn't have the manufacturer's initial on it as all the other pain relief tablets did. The difference was obvious when you were looking for it. But without some good reason to examine the medicine, who would think of doing so?

"We got another one," Jimmy concluded, looking down at Levon.

"Someone else has been drugged?" I asked, trying to keep my voice casual and sort of insinuate the question.

"Yes'm," Jimmy said, not catching the warning look Levon was trying to send him. "Lady last week left her purse in the cart in the grocery while she walked over to the frozen section to get some Ore-Ida hash browns. When she was driving home, she took a pill from a fancy case in her purse, that she used to carry her—well, some prescription medicine—with her. Instead of getting tranquil, she went nuts."

"What did she do?" I asked, fascinated.

"Well…" Jimmy began, treating me to a grin that told me the story was going to be a good one.

"We need to be getting this back to SPACOLEC," Levon said pointedly.

"Huh? Oh, right." Jimmy, aware he'd been on the verge of indiscretion, flushed to the roots of his reddish hair. "When one of Darius's kids shows up, we'll tell them you'd appreciate them moving the truck. The keys were in Darius's pants. I coulda brought 'em out here if you'd mentioned them over the phone."

I flushed guiltily. I'd been so excited over finding the pills, I had forgotten why we'd looked in Darius's truck in the first place.

I watched as their car turned out of our long driveway and began the short stretch into Lawrenceton, piqued that I hadn't gotten to hear the rest of Jimmy's story. I wondered if my friend Sally Allison, a reporter for our local paper, had heard anything.

"I have to go back to the plant for a little while," Martin said unenthusiastically. "I have a stack of letters to sign that need to go out." He climbed back into his car, started it, and rolled down the window as I turned toward the kitchen door. "Don't forget," he called, "we've got dinner at the Lowrys' house tonight." The rain picked up a little momentum.

"I have it on the calendar," I called back, trying not to sound dismal.

If there'd been a can in front of me, I'd have kicked it on my way into the house. It didn't seem like a good night to eat out with people I was (at best) on cordial terms with. Close friends and homemade chili sounded good; friendly acquaintances and dressing up didn't.

Catledge and Ellen Lowry were not soul mates of mine.

But they were among the leading citizens of Lawrenceton. Catledge was the mayor for a second term and Ellen was on every board and a member of every club worth joining in our small town. Keeping the town government, ergo the Lowrys, pleased was important to Martin's business and therefore to a great many people in Lawrenceton who depended on Pan-Am Agra for a paycheck.

"They're not that bad," I said out loud to my silent house. Even to me, I sounded sulky. I trudged upstairs to figure out what to wear, straightening one of the pictures hung by the staircase as I went up. Gradually the house warmed and cheered me, as it nearly always did. My house is at least sixty-five years old, and it has beautiful hardwood floors, tall windows that no standard curtains will fit correctly (so every single "window treatment" has to be custom made), and a voracious appetite for electricity and gas. I love it dearly. We'd had it renovated when we married. Since we've been married less than three years and have no children and only one alleged pet, there's nothing to redo yet; at least not for a basically practical person like me. I still have space on the built-in bookshelves lining the hall, and now I can afford to buy hardbacks.

I showered and shampooed, once again going through the tedious process of combing and drying my mess of hair. At least curly, wavy hair was fashionable now. It was a pleasant change to have others actually envy me my abundance, rather than peer at it with pity in their eyes.

I flipped through the garments in my closet without much interest. The cerise wool dress my mother had brought me was too fancy for the occasion, so I finally decided I'd wear a long-sleeved garnet silk blouse, a black-and-garnet patterned skirt, and my black pumps. Looking at my collection of glasses—I'm very nearsighted—I had a wild impulse to select my purple-and-white-framed ones.

Oh, hell. The Lowrys would be offended if my glasses were frivolous. I got my new black-rimmed ones with the delicate gold wire-and-bead decoration and set them out on my vanity table. This morning I'd put on my favorite workday red specs, and I viewed them in the mirror with some satisfaction. They added a spark of liveliness to my unhappy face.

"So, why'm I sulking?" I asked the mirror.

That particular question never got answered because the front doorbell rang.

What a lot of visitors I was having today, if you counted the deputies coming twice.

Through the opaque oval glass pane in the front door, I saw the silhouette of a woman with a baby carrier in her arms. I assumed it was my friend Lizanne Buckley Sewell, who'd had her baby boy two months before. I disarmed the alarm and opened the door with a smile that collapsed in on itself. I stared blankly at the plump, dark, pretty young woman who stood on my front porch with a perfectly strange baby, who seemed smaller than Lizanne's infant.

"Aunt Roe!" said the dark young woman. She looked exhausted, and she also looked as if she expected a warm welcome.

I had not the slightest idea who she was.

The next instant everything clicked, and I would have

thunked myself on the forehead with the heel of my hand if I'd been alone. I was aunt to only one young woman, and that was Martin's niece, the daughter of his sister Barby.

"Regina!" I said, hoping my recovery hadn't been too obvious.

"For a minute there, I didn't think you recognized me!" she said, laughing.

"Ha, ha. Come on in! And this is little..." Regina had had a baby? It was covered with a blue blanket and wore a red sleeper. Martin had a—great-nephew?

How could I have missed that? Granted, we don't often see Martin's sister and her daughter, but I would have expected a certain amount of phone calling to herald the new arrival.

"Oh, Aunt Roe! This is *Hayden*!"

"And you call him Hayden." I nodded with a wise look. "No nicknames." I could hardly recall ever having been more at sea.

"No, me and Craig are set on him being called Hayden," Regina said, trying to look firm and determined and failing completely.

Martin may not have gotten all the looks in the Bartell family—Barby and Regina are both pretty, in their way—but he'd surely gotten a disproportionate amount of the brains and resolution.

I craned out of the front door, trying to see if Craig Graham was maybe getting luggage out of the trunk. "Where's your husband?" I asked, never imagining this would be a sensitive question.

"He didn't come," Regina said. Her generous mouth clamped tight.

"Oh." I hoped I didn't sound as blank as I felt. "And how's your mother?" I was gesturing to Regina to come on in, still peering around in the hopes of spying a companion. She'd driven all the way from Corinth, Ohio, on her own?

"Mama's on a cruise," Regina said, too gaily. This gal was having serious mood swings.

"Hmmm. Where to?" I repeated my "come in" gesture, more emphatically.

"Oh, she's taking a long one," Regina chattered, finally stepping over the threshold. "The boat stops by some islands in the Caribbean, then over to two stops in Mexico of several days apiece, then back to Miami."

"My goodness," I said mildly. "She's with a friend?"

"That guy," Regina said, depositing the baby, still in his infant seat, on the coffee table in front of the couch and unslinging a huge diaper bag from her shoulder. There was still a fabric-care tag dangling from the shoulder strap of the diaper bag.

"That guy" was Barby's fiancé, investment banker Hubert Morris, whom the divorced Barby Lampton had met when she'd bought a condo in Pittsburgh, the closest major city and airport to Corinth, Ohio, Barby and Martin's childhood home. Though Barby hadn't lived in Corinth since her teenage years, Regina had met her husband-to-be while she and her mother were in Corinth visiting an old friend of Barby's. Regina had married the boy—I mean, young man—only two months later.

Martin and I had flown up to Pittsburgh for the wedding, maybe seven months ago. We'd gotten the impression that the young couple would be living in very straitened circumstances. Craig Graham had been a dark, lanky no-brainer, whose greatest apparent virtue had been that he cared for Regina. He was eighteen to Regina's twenty-one. The groom's share of the wedding duties and expenses had been borne by Barby, who had tried to be unobtrusive about it. Of course, Martin and I had noticed. But Barby had made it clear to us (to Martin, anyway, since she seldom talked to me directly) that after the wedding, the young couple was going to be financially independent, as far as she was concerned. She'd made some pointed remarks about who had made beds and who would be lying in them.

"Would you like a drink? Coffee or hot chocolate? Though maybe those things aren't good for the baby." My friend Lizanne was breast-feeding and, though I hadn't asked, she'd generously given me a *very* thorough grounding on the subject. After being indoctrinated with Lizanne's opinions on the virtues of, and necessity for, mother's milk, I was taken aback when Regina gave me a blank look.

"Huh? No, I'm bottle-feeding," she said, after a pause. "Gosh, if I nursed him, it'd have to be me that fed him every time."

I kept a smile planted on my face. "So, some coffee?"

"Please." She slumped back. "I've been driving for hours."

She *had* driven all the way from Ohio. This was very strange, and getting stranger.

I brewed some coffee, shuddering at Regina's protest that instant would have been fine. After I'd poured a cup for each of us, adding cream and sugar to Martin's niece's,

I listened to Regina blather about the long drive, the baby, her mother's condo, her Aunt Cindy...

"Oh, I'm sorry!" she apologized. "I shouldn't have said anything."

"Aunt Cindy" was Martin's first wife, the mother of his only child, Regina's cousin Barrett. I sighed internally, *still* kept my smile pasted on, and assured Regina that she needn't apologize. A little corner of my brain repressed an urge to ask Regina why she wasn't at Aunt Cindy's instead of Uncle Martin's, if Aunt Cindy was so great.

"Did you see Barrett on TV the other night?" Regina said enthusiastically. "Boy, didn't he look handsome? I always call all my friends when Barrett's going to be on television."

Regina was digging at all my sore—or rather, sensitive—spots. Barrett had not come to our wedding. He'd been up for a big part, he'd told his dad, the implication clear that a new part for Barrett was more important than a new wife for his father.

And he hadn't visited Lawrenceton in the three-plus years Martin had lived here.

But he'd found the time to come to Regina's wedding, where he'd managed to dodge us with an almost unbelievable agility. Martin had told me he'd had a drink with Barrett in the hotel bar after I'd gone up to bed the night before the wedding, and that had been the contact he'd had with his son—whose career he'd been subsidizing.

I was beginning to wish Martin's only niece had stayed in Ohio. I was also beginning to puzzle at the reason behind her visit. She was being mighty evasive.

"Regina," I said, when she'd finished blathering about

Barrett's career, "I'm delighted that you came to visit, but this evening, just for a couple of hours, may be a little awkward. Your uncle and I have a longstanding dinner engagement, and though we could call and tell the Lowrys we have to take a rain check, I'm afraid—"

Regina, who happened to be holding the baby (Hayden, I reminded myself), looked up with something approaching alarm. "You two go on like you had planned. I'll be fine here. Just point me at the microwave and I'll be glad to fix my own supper. After all, I just appeared on your doorstep."

It seemed to me—almost—that Regina was anxious to get us out of the house. I could feel my eyebrows draw together in a frown.

"Excuse me a minute," I said. Regina, her attention focused on the baby, gave me an absent nod.

I went across the hall into the room we'd decorated as a study and a television room. Plucking the cordless phone from its stand, I plumped down on the red leather couch in front of the windows. Madeleine, the cat that lived with us, emerged from her favorite private place, the basket where we put newspapers after we'd read them. While I was punching in numbers with one hand, I was tickling Madeleine's head with the other. One part of my mind noted that I'd have to get Madeleine out of the study before Martin got home. He and the cat enjoyed a hate-hate relationship. It had started with Madeleine deciding Martin's Mercedes was her basking site of choice, especially when the ground was muddy and she could leave some nice footprints on the hood and windshield. Martin had retaliated by parking the Mercedes in the garage and closing the door every night. Since it was then her move in their little game, Madeleine (who ordinarily couldn't be bothered) caught a mouse, decapitated the rodent, and put the corpse in Martin's shoe. Then Martin . . . well, you get the idea.

"Martin Bartell's office," Marnie Sands said. Her raspy voice was all business.

"Mrs. Sands, this is Aurora. I need to speak to Martin." It had taken me weeks to stop apologizing for disturbing him.

"I'm sorry," Mrs. Sands said, her voice several degrees warmer than it had been when I first married Martin, "but Mr. Bartell's out in the plant. Want me to page him?"

I thought of trying to tell Martin that his niece was here with an unexplained baby, over a telephone where he stood surrounded by employees. "No, that's okay," I told the secretary. "Please ask him to call me before he starts for home."

I hung up the phone. I made a face, the kind of face my mother always warned me would make my features stick in permanent disgust.

I strolled back across the hall to Regina. She was putting some bottles of formula in the refrigerator.

"I just made myself at home," she said brightly. She'd gotten out a pan and boiled some water, and an empty can of formula powder was on the counter by the sink. "It always helps to have plenty made up and ready to heat. Now, when I heat them up . . ." and she described the procedure at tedious length.

Hayden stared at me with the big round-eyed goggle some babies have. He was a cute little guy, with a pink mouth and rosy cheeks. In fact, he was strikingly fairer than Regina, who was pretty enough, but endowed with the dark complexion and wide hips her own mother'd bequeathed her. Hayden waved his arms and made a sudden gurgling sound, and Regina looked at him adoringly.

"Isn't he wonderful?" she asked.

"He's so cute," I said, and tried not to sound yearning.

"Too bad Uncle Martin's too old to have another kid," Regina said, actually giggling at the idea.

I could feel my back stiffen and I was sure my face had followed suit.

"We talked about it," I said in a voice of pure ice. "But unfortunately, I am not able." Martin, who was staring fifty in the face, hadn't been able to work up any enthusiasm for starting another family, though at my just-turned birthday of thirty-six, I could still hear my biological clock ticking. Loudly.

However, it was ticking in a malformed womb, which let Martin off the hook as far as making a decision.

I began to empty the dishwasher, all the time telling myself I'd sounded hostile and I had to calm down. Regina, who really seemed to be remarkably tactless, had stuck a sharp stick into my tenderest grievance, my inability to conceive. She was staring at me now, trying to look properly cowed, but I detected a certain—what? Satisfaction? Her eyes had the same look I saw in Madeleine's when she'd left those footprints all over Martin's windshield. I had a sudden inspiration.

"Would it suit you if we put you and Hayden over in the garage apartment?" I asked, trying to make my voice light and friendly.

"That would be super. I wondered when I drove up if that was a separate apartment," Regina said. Maybe she sounded a tad disappointed that I'd changed the subject. "Hayden still gets up at night, and we'd be less likely to bother you."

"Let's just take your things over there," I suggested. Taking the keys from a hook by the back door, I grabbed the big diaper bag and Regina's purse and trotted across the covered walkway and up the stairs that ran up the side of the garage, the side toward our house. The heavy bag looped over my shoulder banged ponderously against my thigh. Though the air was colder and wetter, it wasn't actually raining at the moment.

The apartment smelled only slightly stale. Our friends Shelby and Angel had moved out about eight weeks ago. I had been keeping the heat on so nothing would freeze or mildew, and I turned it up and glanced around as I heard Regina open her car trunk below.

The garage apartment is one very big room, with a corner walled in for a bathroom and adjacent closet. There's a queen-sized bed, a chair and love seat and attendant tables, a television, and a small table for two in the kitchen area. It's as pleasant as basic apartment living gets.

Regina seemed pleased.

"Oh, Aunt Roe, this is so nice," she said, throwing a suitcase on the bed. "Before we got married, we lived in an apartment that was a lot smaller than this."

I hated to think about that.

"Well, I hope you enjoy it," I said at random. "You and Hayden, that is. I'll leave you to unpack. Oh, do you have something for the baby to sleep in?" I had no idea what to do if she didn't. But Regina assured me she had a portable travel crib. That seemed a luxurious item for a poor mother to have, and I wondered a little.

I heard the crunch of gravel as I stood in the doorway. Martin emerged from his car and stood staring at Regina's car for a minute.

"Martin," I called, "come up here." Evidently he hadn't returned to his office before he came home.

He passed under the walkway to stare up at me. "What are you doing in the apartment?" he asked. No one had been in the apartment since Angel and Shelby had bought a house in town.

"Oh," I said, feeling a pleasurable anticipation, perhaps tinged with a touch of malice, "you won't *guess* who's come to visit, honey!"

Looking distinctly apprehensive, Martin came up the stairs. I stood aside so he could enter the apartment.

"Uncle Martin!" cried Regina. She faced the door with a big smile stretching her generous lips, the baby pressed to her chest like a bag of groceries.

Martin's face was priceless.

"Did we know she was coming?" he asked me in a low voice as we walked over to the house.

I shook my head.

"Did we know she'd had a baby?"

I shook my head again.

"Then Barby must not know it either," he said. "She wouldn't keep something like that to herself."

I didn't think so either. I further thought that Barby would just hate the idea of being a grandmother. I was willing to bet Regina knew that, too.

"So, we don't know why she's here?" Martin, used to commanding information and having everything lined up and organized, was definitely on the frustrated side.

"It'd be easier to tell you what I don't know," I said. "I don't know why she came or how long she's staying. I don't know where Craig is. I have no idea what your sister knows." And though I didn't say it out loud to spare Martin's feelings, I was far from certain of the provenance of the baby.

Martin stood in the kitchen drinking a glass of tea while he mulled this over. "I've got to go back up there and speak to her again," he said abruptly. "Get some of this settled. We still going to the Lowrys'?"

"I don't think we can put it off. Regina seems all right about us going, and you know how touchy Catledge is."

"Okay. I'll just be a minute or two with her, then I'll come in and shower." Thunking his glass down on the counter, he marched out again into the gathering dark and dripping rain. His white hair gleamed through the darkness.

I went upstairs to finish getting ready. As I put on makeup and jewelry and pinned my hair out of my face with a pretty black-and-gold comb, I wondered if Martin would be able to winkle any more out of his niece than I had. Martin is far more likely to ask direct questions than I am.

But he didn't look satisfied when he trudged up the stairs twenty minutes later. He looked tired and worried.

After giving me a quick kiss on the neck, Martin unzipped his pants and sat on the bed to untie his shoes.

"Hey, sailor, how about it?" I asked, in my best Mae West voice.

Martin flashed me a smile. He glanced at the bedside clock. "Afraid we don't have time," he said regretfully. "I have to shower. Two people in the meeting smoked."

Martin hates the smell of smoke clinging to his hair and clothes.

"You could have asked them not to," I said mildly. Martin's asking might as well be called telling: He was the boss.

"They're going to retire at the new year," he said. "If that weren't the case, I would have kicked their asses out into the hall. As of January one, I'm going to make the entire plant a smoke-free zone."

We talked about how many smokers Pan-Am Agra employed, and mulled over other mundane topics as Martin stripped, showered, and re-dressed. Martin is almost thirteen years my senior, but he looks absolutely great without his clothes on, and he's just as attractive dressed. He has snowy white hair, but his eyebrows are still black, and his eyes are a light, light brown. He lifts weights and his racquetball games are endurance tests for the younger members of the management staff.

"Didn't you say you had your physical today?" Looking at Martin's physique had prompted another train of thought.

"Yes," he said, rather shortly. My wifely antennae perked, tuned in to what he wasn't saying.

"Wasn't everything all right?" Martin had never had a

bad physical. In fact, he was usually boastful after his annual checkup, required by the plant.

"Zelman wants me to have a full battery of tests. Just because I'm getting older," Martin added hastily, before I could even fully develop my concerned expression.

"Did he find anything?" I asked, in the voice that said he better let me know everything.

"He said I was stressed. He just wants to run some more tests." Martin was standing in front of his closet picking out his clothes for the evening. I understood from his tone that the subject was closed.

"We'll schedule those right away," I suggested.

"Sure, I'll get Mrs. Sands to do it tomorrow. Did I tell you she's going to be a grandmother?"

"Is she happy about it?"

"Oh, yes, she's already named the baby and picked out a preschool. Not that her daughter knows about that..."

All this chatter was a delaying tactic of Martin's, while he thought over whatever Regina had told him.

"What'd Regina say?" I asked, as he used his electric razor.

"Not much," he admitted, sticking out his chin to shave under it. I was sitting on the toilet lid. Not for the first time, it occurred to me how much I enjoyed being married, just sitting in the bathroom with a man while he shaved, and all the little intimacies that entailed. "I don't think she's going to tell us why she's here until she's ready." He stretched his upper lip down over his front teeth. "I hope nothing's happened to Craig."

"If he'd been in a wreck or been ill, surely she'd let us know," I said hesitantly, aware I wasn't on Martin's wavelength.

"I was thinking more of Craig being in trouble," he said, pulling on a fresh shirt and tucking it in. "Do you have your lipstick on yet?"

"No," I said, surprised.

Martin pulled me to him and gave me one of those wonderful kisses that makes my pulse jump around like a drop of oil in a hot skillet. I responded enthusiastically, and let my fingers do the walking.

"Whoa! Whoa!" he said, gasping, holding me away. "Oh, later! After we come home!"

"That better be a promise," I said lightly, giving him a final pat and sitting at my vanity to twist the tube to apply Mad Rubies.

"Take it as sworn to," he told me.

We should have taken twenty extra minutes and been late to the Lowrys'.

2

Catledge Lowry met us at the door, his wide happy smile fixed in place.

Catledge was a politician through and through. He had a good-sounding set of goals, he had a good campaign manager, and he'd done some worthwhile things. I didn't trust him as far as I could throw him, and given Catledge's six-foot-four frame, that wasn't an inch. I just enjoyed Catledge for what he was.

"Hey, good lookin'!" he cried. "If your husband would just turn his back a minute, I'd give you a kiss to curl your toes, you beautiful thing!"

"This beautiful thing would rather have a glass of wine, Catledge," I said, smiling. "Besides, I don't think you can bend down far enough." I'm four-eleven.

"Honey, I'd amputate my legs for the chance," Catledge said dramatically, and I laughed.

"Ellen might not care for that," I said, handing him my coat. Martin reached past me to shake hands, and in a moment the men were deep in conversation about some yahoo's chance in the Georgia governor's race. I expected a flushed and harried Ellen to rush from the kitchen, but instead I saw her strolling through the garage door holding a brown paper bag containing, from its shape, a bottle of wine. She was groomed to a tee and in no great hurry, either. I had a moment of surprise and then Ellen was bending down to peck my cheek, and I was reconnecting with the bundle of nerves that was Ellen Dawson Lowry.

Ellen was maybe five-ten, as tall as Martin, and thin as a rail. She dressed beautifully, used minimal makeup, would be an unobtrusive blonde for the next twenty years with a little help, and had graduated with honors from Sophie Newcomb. She'd intended to be a CPA. Then she'd married Catledge, and all her mild ambition had been consumed in Catledge's flashy brilliance.

Ellen had told me she'd been happy when their sons had been young, and happy when she worked at the bank for a few years while the boys were in high school; but Catledge had wanted her to quit when he'd been elected mayor, and she had. At one time, when we'd had to work together on the board of a charity, we'd felt rather close. But after our year on the board was up, it had seemed harder and harder for us to meet, and our brief closeness faded.

"Roe, you just get prettier and prettier!" Ellen gushed.

"Oh, Ellen," I mumbled, embarrassed at her strange manner.

Ellen's eyes had a glaze to them, and her hands moved nervously up and down the skirt of the dark blue-and-gold dress. The colors were becoming, but Ellen had lost even more weight and looked almost painfully thin.

"What do you hear from your boys?" I asked.

"Jefferson's tenth in the senior class at Georgia Tech, and Tally is… working on a special study in Tennessee." Despite her hesitation over nineteen-year-old Tally's current occupation, Ellen was like most mothers in her pleasure in talking about her children, and my questions kept our conversation rolling along until Mrs. Esther came in to announce dinner. Martin and I exchanged discreet glances.

Lucinda Esther is a notable personality in Lawrenceton, and the fact that the Lowrys had hired her to produce this meal surprised us. This was not a dinner on which some important deal depended; this was not a crucial social event. Hiring Mrs. Esther always signaled that the meal was significant, perhaps when the parents of the bride entertained the parents of the groom for the first time, or when an important newcomer was welcomed into an affluent home.

Maybe, in this instance, it meant the hostess was not capable of producing a suitable meal.

Standing with massive dignity in a starched gray uniform with a white apron, Mrs. Esther said, "Dinner is served." She did not meet our eyes or wait for a reaction, but strode back into the kitchen, her dark face still impassive, her chin proudly up. The heavy gold hoops in her pierced ears swayed as she walked.

Mrs. Esther didn't serve. She placed the food ready on the table and remained in the kitchen until it was time to clean up. And she almost always prepared a menu she'd decided on herself. Tonight she'd picked chicken baked in a white sauce, green beans, homemade rolls, sweet potato casserole, and a tossed salad. Calories and cholesterol were not considerations in Mrs. Esther's catering business.

After we'd all passed the dishes around, which was a pretty effective icebreaker, Martin asked me to tell Catledge what had happened in our backyard that afternoon.

As I turned it into an amusing vignette, without the element of anxiety that had given the incident its edge, naturally I glanced from Catledge to Ellen and back. Catledge was at the end of the table to my left and Ellen was opposite me. Their reactions were more intriguing than the story. Catledge was shaken, visibly upset; Ellen thought the whole episode was vastly amusing. I'd have sworn Catledge would laugh and Ellen would worry. This reversal was very interesting.

To my further fascination, Catledge cut the ensuing discussion off at the knees. I was just sure as sure can be that ordinarily Catledge would spend a good fifteen minutes speculating about who'd "spiked" Darius Quattermain's acetaminophen. Yet here he was, trying to shunt the conversation into the ongoing battle between two factions of the library board. I shot a significant look at Martin while Ellen was fetching more tea from the kitchen and Catledge had excused himself.

I can't let puzzling behavior go by without picking it apart to discover its cause. Suddenly I wondered if Ellen had been the unnamed woman who'd been sabotaged by the medicine switcher.

I was pleased with the idea, the more I hammered it out. Twitchy Ellen was very likely to have tranquilizers in her purse. She was certainly abnormally serene tonight. Perhaps Catledge feared staying on the subject of Darius Quattermain because he thought Ellen likely to reveal her own little episode of similarly bizarre behavior? He would hate it to be known Ellen took "nerve pills."

The silence that had fallen over the dinner table was so awkward that Martin felt compelled to break it.

"We had a surprise visitor today," he said easily.

"Who was that?" Catledge asked, right on cue, relief easy to read in his voice.

"My niece came to visit, with her baby boy," Martin said.

I cocked an eyebrow at him. We weren't going to mention Regina's visit, we'd decided.

"A boy," Ellen said. "I miss our boys. They were adorable babies. But all cute babies grow up and leave home, don't they?" That should have been said in a light tone, but it wasn't. Ellen's voice grew more and more edgy with every word. Once again, an uneasy silence fell over the table.

Ellen pushed her chair back and rose, maybe a little unsteadily. "Excuse me, please," she said, managing to sound almost normal. "I'm being a bad hostess. I feel unwell." And walking quickly, her backbone stiff, she was out of the room and going up the stairs, face carefully turned away.

"I'm so sorry Ellen is ill," I said instantly. "She should have canceled. We would have understood. Bless her heart, she worked so hard when she should have been in bed." I hoped my chatter would fill the silence and smooth things over, and to some extent it did.

"Ellen never knows when to take things easy," Catledge said gratefully. "We'd love to have you back when she's well."

"Oh, no, it's our turn," Martin contributed. He was already up and retrieving my coat. "We enjoyed the evening, I'm just sorry it ended this way."

As Martin and Catledge kept up the social end of the evening, I stepped into the kitchen to tell Mrs. Esther that I'd enjoyed the food and that she could clear the table.

Mrs. Esther was sitting at the small breakfast table in the bay window in the kitchen reading *How Stella Got Her Groove Back.* Just as I opened my mouth to speak, I saw that the kitchen door to the garage was being pulled shut, and I understood that Ellen had gone down the back stairs, stepped silently through the kitchen, and—this I definitely heard—was starting up the car in the garage.

When I looked from the garage door back to Mrs. Esther, I saw that she was regarding me with an absolutely neutral expression. As clearly as if she'd spoken it, her face said, "This is none of my business and I don't want to know."

"Thanks for the delicious supper, Mrs. Esther," I said. I picked a dish at random. "The chicken was especially good."

"Thank you, Mrs. Bartell." Another one who didn't call me Ms. Teagarden. But it was not an issue I was going to fight over. It had never made any difference to me what people called me, as long as I knew who I was.

We exchanged good-byes, and I turned back to the dining room to find Martin and Catledge shaking hands. But then Catledge mentioned the Wednesday meeting of the zoning commission, and Martin remembered that Pan-Am Agra had bought some land adjacent to the plant that needed to be rezoned, and they started up all over again.

I couldn't fiddle with the table, not with Mrs. Esther in the kitchen waiting to take care of it, and I couldn't wander around the house because that would be rude. So I fished around in my purse for a mint and surreptitiously popped it into my mouth, I got all my hair freed from the collar of my coat, and then I gently patted Martin's arm.

"You and Catledge will just have to call each other tomorrow, honey. We need to get home."

Martin smiled down at me fondly. "You're right, Roe. We need to check on Regina and the baby before we turn in."

So, finally, finally, we were out the door and on our way. Even then, we had to stop to get gas, because Martin was low and didn't want to have to fill up on the way to work in the morning.

We'd had Ellen's wine with our meal, and a somewhat trying day, so we were quiet and (speaking for myself) sleepy on the drive home. Though I was still mildly concerned about Regina's visit and the unexplained baby, I was willing to put off worrying about it until the next morning. But I could tell from Martin's frown that he was brooding over it again.

As we turned up our long driveway, my pleasant drowsiness evaporated.

Though I couldn't tell much about it, there was a strange car parked in front of the garage. And Regina's car was gone.

The automatic security light at the back of the house showed, also, that someone had taken Darius's truck and trailer. I hoped it was one of his children.

We didn't have an automatic security light at the front of the house because it had shone in our bedroom window; we'd had it switched to manual, and we'd forgotten to leave it on when we'd left for the Lowrys' dinner. The brilliant light in the backyard gave the front some illumination, but it was faint and full of shadows.

So the front of the house and garage was relatively dark... but aside from the strange car and absence of Regina's, there was plenty visible to alarm us. I could see, and so could Martin by his grunt, that there was something lying on the stairs that mounted to the garage apartment.

Most worrying of all was the irregular fan of dark spots on the white siding of the garage.

"Martin," I said sharply, as if he hadn't already noticed all these things for himself. We looked at each other as he switched off the Mercedes's engine.

"Stay here," he said firmly, and opened his door.

"No," I said, and opened mine. The cat was crouched in the azaleas, staring at the thing on the stairs. Madeleine didn't acknowledge our presence; she remained fixed and alert in her chosen spot. Somehow that made my skin crawl, and for the first time I was convinced this might be something bad, very bad.

It wasn't just very bad. It was absolutely horrible.

The dark stain on the white siding was a spray of blood. As I stared at it, one drop moved. Not completely dry.

The blood had shot from the long limp thing on the stairs, a man.

A hatchet had cleaved through his forehead. It was still embedded in his head. Blood had soaked into the dark hair. I thought about Regina and the baby, and if your heart could actually move within your body, mine would have fallen to the pit of my stomach. I suspected the dead man was Craig, Regina's husband.

Martin was looking up the stairs to the apartment door. There was a line of black where it should have met the frame. The door was ajar.

That realization was enough to propel me over to my husband. In the dim light, I could see that he looked old and ill, all the lines time had ironed into his face seeming deeper in the shadows. And since I knew him, I knew he was thinking he had to go up those stairs and find out what was in that apartment. But he was afraid of what he'd find. Regina and her baby were his family.

A light rain began to pelt down.

Wordlessly, I laid my hand on Martin's shoulder and squeezed it before edging by the dead thing sprawled on the stairs. I tried not to look down as I sidled up with my back to the railing. I didn't want to touch the blood on the wall, either. Once past the body, I went faster, but still my legs were heavy with reluctance and quivering with fear. It seemed an hour before I faced the door.

There was a little sound inside the apartment.

I bit down hard on my lip. I poked the door open with one fingertip. Reaching in, I flipped up the light switch by the door. A brilliant glare illuminated the apartment. I spent a long moment scanning for Regina's body, bloodstains, signs of a struggle.

Nothing.

The little sound went on and on.

Finally I stepped in, looking repeatedly from side to side. Martin called from below, but I didn't answer. My breath was coming too unevenly. The rain began to fall more heavily and the drumming of the raindrops on the stairs made the little apartment feel more isolated.

The closet door was open. Clothes, I assumed Regina's, had been hung inside. Her suitcase was on the dining table, open. Clothes that appeared to have been tossed in rather than packed were flowing over the sides. The bathroom door was flung wide and I could see a jumble of makeup and toiletries on the counter by the sink.

The only area not visible from my position by the door was the floor on the far side of the bed. And that was where the sound was coming from.

I went around the bed, reasoning with one part of my mind that nothing could be worse than what I had already seen.

The floor was empty, but the folds of the quilted paisley bedspread were moving, down at carpet level. I dropped to my knees and bent over. Holding my breath, I lifted the skirt of the bedspread.

Under the bed, kicking his legs and waving his hands, was the baby. He was just beginning to get upset that his mother hadn't picked him up after his nap. He looked perfectly all right, and his red sleeper was pristine.

So Regina's car was missing, and Regina wasn't anywhere in the apartment.

I was certainly thinking without clarity. At first, I thought the baby's presence and wellness were good news. And they were good news, of course, but they were only part of Martin's concern. When I came to the top of the stairs and called down to him that the baby was fine but Regina was gone, the look on his face reminded me that someone had murdered the young man on the stairs, and the vanished Regina was by far the most likely person to have wielded the hatchet. Martin was standing passively, leaning against the garage, his arms crossed over his chest. His hair and his coat were dark with rain. His alien behavior struck me like a fist to the chest.

"You have to call the police," I reminded him, and I saw

the anger flare in my husband's face. He didn't like being told to do that. My presence obliged him to do the right thing. He'd been thinking of concealing this somehow, I could tell. It was the pirate side of him coming out.

There was something stuck under the windshield wiper blade of the strange car, which I noticed had Ohio tags. I could hardly get much wetter, so I carefully eased down the stairs and over to the car. I touched the sodden mass with a finger. It was a folded piece of paper, a note. I could see the streaks that had been blue ink. A note: to whom, about what, I'd never know.

The baby began to scream. His cries carried on the chilly night air. I expected someone to pick him up and tend to his needs, and when that didn't happen, I had what Lizanne calls a Real Moment. Hayden's mother had vanished; Hayden's father, Craig (and I was pretty sure the corpse was Craig, though I'd only met him once at the wedding), was lying before me dead. The baby's grandmother, who ought to be willing to take charge, was on a cruise with her boyfriend. I, Aurora Teagarden, was (at least temporarily) responsible for this baby, unless Martin acted. Staring at my husband, I saw how unlikely that was. Instead of feeling elation—finally, a baby!—I felt an almost bottomless dismay.

The rain pattered to a halt.

I turned and once again mounted the stairs to the garage apartment. I squatted and eased Hayden out from under the bed. With effort, I rose from the floor holding him. It was shocking how much he could wiggle, how hard it was to hold on to him, especially when he arched his body with rage. I was trembling, and it wasn't for the dead man on the stairs. Somehow, I made it down the stairs and across the walkway, passing a still-silent Martin without saying anything.

After unlocking our house, I reached for the security pad, only to find that it had been turned off. Of course, we hadn't told Regina how to set it . . . at least, I hadn't. I called 911 from our kitchen telephone. I jiggled Hayden with one damp arm while I dialed with my free hand. I could barely hold him, but I couldn't put him on the kitchen floor. He was screaming so loudly by now that I had to repeat myself twice. At least Doris wasn't still on duty, and the dispatcher didn't seem to know that I'd already had county police at my house that day. After I hung up, I could put off tending to Hayden no longer.

I had no idea what to do.

As Hayden's need, whatever it was, wasn't met, he screamed more. Too frightened and uncertain to leave him by himself, I staggered back out into the night, toting the increasingly heavy baby, and edged once again past the awful thing on the stairs. Its horror was actually paling in comparison to my frenzied desire for Hayden to shut up.

I wished Martin would stir himself to help me, but he was standing with his hands on the Mercedes hood, looking out into the night, that odd introspective look still on his face.

The baby's diaper bag, feeling considerably lighter, was lying on its side in the middle of the floor. I was glad to see it. I looped the strap over my shoulder and carried the shrieking Hayden on yet another trek into our house. I was utterly unable to think of what to do next.

But Hayden wouldn't stop crying.

I tried to reason through all the noise. He must be wet or hungry, right? Or both. Wasn't that generally what was wrong with babies?

I opened his diaper bag and pulled out one of the disposable diapers Regina used. Then I had to figure it out, since I'd never even examined such an item, much less put one on a baby.

When I thought I understood the thing, I ripped a paper towel off the roll and spread it on the kitchen table, where we ate most of our meals. I plopped Hayden down on the middle of the towel and began to unsnap his sleeper, which seemed incredibly complicated. I extricated his kicking legs with great difficulty and peeled open the tabs holding the diaper shut.

Whew. He did need a fresh one.

I had to clean him off. What with? I couldn't take my hands off him. What if he rolled off the table? This problem absorbed me so thoroughly that the sirens of the arriving cars were only background noise. My free hand found a plastic box in the diaper bag. I flipped it open and found premoistened towelettes inside. Yahoo!

After a few more strenuous minutes, Hayden was clean and rediapered... more or less. He was whimpering now, and I knew he'd break out into screaming again if I didn't solve whatever other problems he had. Hunger seemed the most likely, and I remembered Regina preparing the bottles that afternoon. God bless her, I thought. If she left me bottles for this baby I'll forgive her, no matter what else she has done.

There were four bottles in the refrigerator. I heated one up in the microwave as Regina had shown me, and I wondered if she had foreseen her departure when she made such a point of telling me how to prepare the bottles, how to test them for temperature.

The idea that Regina might have known she'd be leaving was so unpleasant I was sorry I'd thought of it. I put Hayden in his infant seat, which I found in the living room and carried back into the kitchen, and held his bottle to his mouth. Hayden did the rest. I slumped in a chair, my forehead resting on my hand, my other hand holding the bottle in the right position (I hoped).

I heard feet tramping up the steps to the kitchen door, and I knew it was time to answer questions. I looked down at Hayden, who was pulling on the bottle as if it were the answer to all the troubles of the universe.

I wished I could have one.

3

After an hour or two of the county cops coming in and out, I was so exhausted, angry, and horrified that I could hardly put two words together, much less come up with coherent answers. Martin was outside most of the time, but he came through the kitchen with Sheriff Padgett Lanier following close on his heels. They went into the study across the hall and didn't come out for ages.

I passed the dreary time trying to resnap Hayden's sleeper, holding him, and trying to burp him, something I recollected you were supposed to do to babies after you fed them.

"You need to hold him up a little," said one husky young man in the khaki of the sheriff's department. "I got a four-month-old," he added, to establish his credentials. I shifted the warm bundle cautiously, offering it to him.

"And you need to have a diaper over your shoulder," he continued helpfully. I passed him a cloth diaper from the bag just in time. Hayden smiled and burped formula all over the diaper. The young man smiled back at him and handed the child to me. I held out my arms reluctantly. I was unused to the baby's weight, and my shoulders were already aching.

Then I was horrified by how spoiled I must be, since I realized I was angry at Martin because he was not somehow making this baby go away, or at least commiserating with me, or at the *very* least giving me tips on what to do, because after all, he'd had one.

I resolutely made myself feel sympathy for Martin, who had found a horribly dead man on our property, who was missing a niece suspected of murder, who wasn't able to contact his sister and let her know about this situation; and on top of it all, he was still in wet clothes.

Once I rose out of my snit and channeled my thoughts in less emotional directions, I asked myself the obvious question: Was the dead man really Craig, Regina's husband? I hadn't seen Craig since the wedding. The dead man had been wearing jeans, a leather jacket... I couldn't remember any more than that, but I knew I'd see his face again in my dreams.

When I mentioned the soggy note under the windshield wiper to one of the officers who passed back and forth in a steady stream, he said it had disintegrated when they'd tried to extricate it.

Gradually all the men and women left, and all the cars reversed, and I understood that the body had been removed and the last question had been asked. At least for tonight. I looked up at the clock. It was midnight, only two and a half hours since we'd left the Lowrys' house. Hayden had at last gone to sleep, and I'd put him in the infant seat, grateful for the chance to rest my arms, which were definitely worn out from the unaccustomed burden.

I put my head down on the table. I must have dozed. When I looked at the clock again, it read twelve-thirty. Martin was standing by the table, looking at me.

"Let's go to bed," he said, his voice empty.

"We have to get the portable crib for the baby," I pointed out, trying to sound practical rather than aggrieved.

He stared at Hayden almost in astonishment, as if he'd assumed the police had taken the baby with them, too.

"Oh my God," he said wearily.

I bit my tongue to keep from speaking.

After what I considered more than enough time for him to volunteer, I said in a tight voice, "If you'll keep an eye on him, I'll go get it."

"Okay," said Martin, to my complete amazement. He sat in another chair and propped his chin on his hand, looking at the baby's face as if he'd never seen one.

Gritting my teeth and simply ducking under the crime scene tape, I went up those apartment stairs once more, maneuvering carefully around the bloodstains and wondering who the hell would clean them up. Probably me, I figured. I was building up a good head of grievance.

It was a shock to see how messy the apartment was. Of course, they'd searched for evidence about the crime and Regina's whereabouts. I don't know why I'd assumed they'd leave it neat. I shook my head in disgust with my own naiveté and snatched up a flattened contraption I assumed was the portable crib. There were assembly directions on a white rectangle attached to the pastel bumper sort of thing. I was pathetically grateful.

I was so scared I wouldn't hear the baby if he woke in the night that I laboriously assembled the crib right by our bed.

Martin didn't comment. At least he carried the diaper bag up after me, and at least I managed to lay Hayden down without waking him. I perceived Hayden as a baby—instead of a massive problem—for one moment before exhaustion took over; for that moment, I saw the smooth pale skin, the tiny fingers, the sweet crease of the neck, and it took my breath away.

Then he was once more a terrifyingly fragile being, who was (it seemed) my sole responsibility, and I was totally ignorant of how to take care of him. I sighed, pulled off my clothes, and tossed them into the wicker basket in the bathroom. I pulled on my blue nightgown, brushed my teeth, and sank into bed. I registered that Martin was turning out the light before I retreated into sleep.

"Was it our hatchet?" Martin was asking me.

"Uhmm?"

"Roe, was that our hatchet?"

I considered, my head still pillowed on my arms. I felt warm and comfortable, but as soon as I really woke, misery was just waiting to pounce.

I rolled over, snuggled up to my husband.

"I don't know," I said against his chest. Martin sleeps in pajama bottoms only.

He put his arm around me absently, his chin gently rubbing the top of my head. "I hope it wasn't," was all he said.

"She didn't do it."

"Why do you think that?" He didn't sound upset, just curious.

"She wouldn't leave her baby, right? And she wouldn't leave all her stuff, either," I said more firmly.

"But her car is gone, not the one Craig came in."

"That was Craig's car?" Martin didn't bother answering. Of course, Craig had gotten here somehow; he hadn't dropped from the sky.

Not that the scenario was unknown to me; a body had dropped from the sky into my garden the year before. But it seemed unlikely it would happen twice, even to me.

So, I reasoned, Craig had come after Regina. He'd been in his own car. Maybe Regina had left him and Craig wanted her to come back. They quarreled and Regina took the hatchet that… How did the hatchet enter the picture? Where had it been before it landed in the middle of Craig's forehead?

Okay, ignore that mental image. Say Craig had been threatening Regina with a hatchet he'd gotten out of his own car—"Come back to me or I'll kill you"—and she got it away from him and killed him with it.

While he stood passively below her on the stairs?

And then she wrote a note to her uncle and fled, leaving her baby to the care of whoever walked in the apartment door?

Okay.

Craig had brought a friend with him, who had taken a letch to Regina. This friend got a hatchet and killed Craig and abducted Regina, but didn't want to be burdened with Hayden. Or the friend didn't even know there was a baby, so to save the child, Regina had snatched a moment to stash Hayden under the bed.

I thought that scenario covered everything. I relayed my theory to Martin.

"That would exonerate Regina," he said, sounding as

if that were a very remote possibility. He seemed a smidge more hopeful, though. "I'm sure she left because someone forced her to. I can't believe she'd leave the baby unless she was under duress." Martin kissed my forehead to say thank you, but the arm beneath my neck felt like a log, it was so hard with tension.

I decided to relieve his stress in the happiest way. I nuzzled his nipple. He drew in his breath sharply and his unoccupied hand found something pleasant to do.

"Eh!" said a little voice behind me.

I shrieked.

"It's the baby," Martin said, after a fraught moment. "In the crib. By the bed."

"Eh!" said Hayden. I rolled over to see two tiny hands waving in the air.

"Oh, no no no," I moaned, all thoughts of sex flying out of my head like rats leaving a sinking ship. "I don't know what to do. You had a baby, you have to help."

"Cindy took care of Barrett when he was a baby."

Why was I not surprised?

"I was always . . . too scared to do things for him. He was so little. He was three weeks premature. And by the time he was large enough, when I was sure I couldn't hurt him by accident, Cindy and I had gotten into the habit of her taking care of him, bathing and feeding and diapering."

Absurdly, it was not Martin's ignorance of baby care that made tears spring to my eyes as I dragged myself from the bed. It was the thought of Martin and Cindy's shared experiences: the birth of Barrett, the concern about his health and fears for his survival after the premature birth, his slow growth and improvement with Martin and Cindy watching as parents. All this he'd had with her, and would never have with me.

I hadn't ever been jealous of Cindy before, and I'd certainly picked a bad time to start.

Already feeling tired, I hoisted Hayden from his portable crib—surely he'd gained weight during the night?—and laid him on the bed beside Martin while I found my bathrobe. When I turned back, Martin was propped up on one elbow, looking down at the baby, his finger extended for Hayden to grasp. The baby was regarding Martin solemnly. I stood for a long moment looking, feeling my heart break along several different fault lines.

I turned away to pull my mass of wavy hair back into a ponytail and secure it. Hayden had showed a tendency to grab and pull the night before, and I hadn't enjoyed the experience. I tied the sash of the black velour robe and cautiously bent down to lift the infant from the bed.

"How old do you reckon he is?" I asked, startled to think I didn't even know this child's age.

"I have no idea." Martin stared at the baby, running some comparisons in his head. "He seems a little smaller than Bubba and Lizanne's kid."

He did to me, too. "Maybe—a month?" I hazarded.

He shrugged his bare shoulders.

"People will ask," I said, and to my own ears I already sounded tired. "People always do."

"Oh, God." Martin rolled onto his back, pressing his hands against his face as if to guard it from the world.

"You'd better call Cindy," I said, trying to sound matter-of-fact. "Regina halfway implied they were close. Maybe she can tell us some more about this baby. Maybe she knows how to contact Barby."

I went down the stairs carefully, holding up the nightgown and bathrobe with one hand while pressing Hayden to me with my free arm. I was relieved when I reached the bottom safely, and felt foolishly optimistic at this good omen.

There was a discreet tap at the kitchen door. Now, this knock was unmistakable. My mother.

I canceled the security and opened the door.

My mother, Aida Brattle Teagarden Queensland, is fifty-seven and stunning. She is Lauren Bacall on a good day. She is sharp, smart, and by her own efforts has amassed a small fortune. I love her. She loves me. We live on different planets.

"Have they found the girl?" Mother stepped inside.

"The girl" would be Regina. "No. Not that we know of. I just got up," I explained unnecessarily.

"Martin still in bed?" She glanced up at the clock. It was already nine-thirty.

"We had a late night," I reminded her. I'd called Mother as soon as I could after the police arrived so she wouldn't hear our news from someone else.

Mother held out her arms and made a peremptory gesture. I gave her the baby. Mother had three step grandchildren now, and to my amazement she was very fond of them.

Mother looked down at the boy, who looked back, for a wonder in silence.

"Maybe two, three weeks old," she said briefly, and put him in his infant seat, still in the middle of the table. "Got formula?"

"Regina mixed some up before she..." I trailed off into confusion. Before she murdered her husband and ran? Before she was abducted by aliens?

"You need a nurse for that baby," my mother observed. Her voice was absolutely matter-of-fact; she judged me totally incompetent at child care, which wounded me somehow. But then, why should she have any faith in my ability to take care of a baby? I never had before.

It was funny what hurt and what bounced off. This really hurt.

"You'd better call your friends and see if you can find a temporary babysitter," Mother suggested.

I stared at her. She wasn't offering to do it for me, or rather to have her office manager do it? It dawned on me that all was not well with Mother. I'd been so absorbed in my own problems that I hadn't even looked at her with much attention.

"What's wrong?" I asked. I hated the quaver in my voice.

"John had a mild... well, maybe a heart attack last night, about two hours after you called," she said.

"Oh, no," I said, my eyes filling with tears immediately. I was fond of John Queensland, having been his friend before he dated and married my mother. I took a deep breath. Mother wasn't crying, so I couldn't cry. "How is he doing?"

"I've moved him to Atlanta. They're doing tests right now," she said, and I could read the exhaustion in her face, and the fear.

"I'm so sorry," I said quietly. "What can I do to help you?"

"You have your hands full," she said, looking out the kitchen window. It was another windy, overcast day; a leaf from the gum tree whirled past. "It's just a lot of hospital sitting, and you can't help me sit."

I thought of Martin, the baby, the missing woman, the dead man.

My mother finally needed me and I couldn't help.

"Are Avery and John David there?" I asked. These were John's two sons, both in their thirties and married.

"John David flies in this morning. Melinda's going to meet him at the airport and get him to the hospital. That's something she can do with the kids in the car," she said. Mother smiled briefly, and I saw with a kind of unworthy pang that she had become very fond of Melinda, Avery's wife.

"What's the prognosis?" I asked, dreading the answer. Behind her back I noticed Martin standing in the doorway. I didn't know how long he'd been there.

"We don't know yet," Mother said quietly. "He's been conscious, off and on. He's in some pain."

"Don't worry about us, Aida," my husband said. He moved until he was by Mother's side, and he gripped her shoulder. Her hand came up briefly to cover his, and then they both retreated back into more comfortable personas. "We'll be fine, we just have to get this straightened out."

"Roe," Mother said, as she picked up her purse and went to the door. "This is just an *awful lot* of trouble at one time."

I realized she was half apologizing for focusing on her husband, or at least extending her regrets that my trouble was not her only concern.

"We'll all get through it," I said briskly, trying not to

cry. "I'll be checking with you later. Tell John I'm thinking of him."

She nodded. She'd scrawled John's hospital room phone number on a sheet of paper, and she handed it to me.

After Mother left, I sank down into a chair and put my head in my hands. If the baby started crying, I just couldn't bear it.

The baby started crying.

I forced myself up and to the refrigerator, thinking (as I pulled a bottle from the shelf and popped it into the microwave) that I was almost willing to forgive Regina for everything if she would just return and leave again with the baby.

Martin had made coffee. I noticed he was dressed in khakis and a sweater, about as casual as Martin gets in day wear. He was staring out the window sipping from a mug, looking like a Lands' End ad. I was still in my velour robe, my hair was trailing down my back in a cascade of waves and tangles, and I was in a very tense mood. Hayden, still dressed in the same red sleeper and a diaper that was undoubtedly dirty, was yelling.

"Pick up the baby," I said to Martin.

"What?" he said, turning to me with an automatic smile. "I can't hear you, the baby's crying."

I hadn't had a cup of coffee.

"Pick . . . up . . . the . . . baby," I said.

Martin was so surprised he put down his mug and picked up the baby.

I took the bottle from the microwave and shook it. I tested some formula on my arm. It was the right temperature, as far as I could tell. I handed the bottle to Martin, who had to free his left hand to take it.

I left the room.

I stomped across the hall, or at least I tried to, but stomping is uphill work in fuzzy slippers. I stuck John's hospital phone number by the desk telephone. I flung myself down sideways on the red leather sofa, my back braced against one armrest, and stared out the window at the nasty gray cold windy day. That was exactly how I felt inside, I fumed, nasty and cold and gray. Maybe not *windy*... Then all my rage turned into something much more immediate as a head appeared between the back of the couch and the window. It was the head of a young man, a blond and handsome young man, and his expression was groggy.

"Hey," he said. "You're Aunty Roe? I thought you'd be old. Where's the kid?"

I shrieked and set a record for bounding off red leather couches.

Martin was hampered in his rescue attempt by the baby. He looked ready for action when he appeared in the doorway, but the effect was spoiled by the feeding Hayden. Martin shoved baby and bottle into my arms and stood waiting. He was spoiling for a fight, which the young man was just perceptive enough to see.

"Hey, man, it's okay, didn't Regina tell you I was here?"

We stared at him.

It gradually sank into his dim consciousness that something was drastically wrong.

"So, where's Craig?" he asked uncertainly, working his way out from behind the couch. He proved to be not much over five-eight, and he was wearing ancient blue jeans and a none-too-clean flannel shirt hanging open over a T-shirt. A golden stubble made his face look dirty. But he didn't look threatening. He had an aura of amiable stupidity that I came to learn was, to some extent, quite accurate.

Martin and I exchanged glances.

"Did you come here with Craig?" Martin asked, as if the answer were not important.

"Sure, didn't he tell you?"

"Was Regina expecting you?" I asked next.

"Well, no. She didn't expect Craig to get out early, but the jail got real crowded, and Craig really toes the line when he's in, so they released him early."

There was so much in this sentence to absorb that we just stood and stared. Visibly unnerved, the stranger tried to fill the silence with chatter. "See, after we stopped for some beer at that liquor store on the main drag, we had to help this lady who was having trouble with her car. And then we got here, but all of a sudden I was feeling really really tired. I never felt anything like that. So we came over here to this house, and Regina was in the kitchen with the baby, and she and Craig started fighting right away, you know, and I could see this couch across the hall while I was standing there listening to them, and I was so sleepy I just came in here and lay down. That's the last I remember, except I had a dream about hearing someone scream, and I musta hid."

We exchanged glances again.

"Ain't you ever going to say nothing? You are Regina's aunt and uncle, right? Though I got to say, lady, you don't look old enough to be anyone's aunt." He grinned at me, or tried to, but by now it was so obvious something was wrong that his grin was only a shadow of what it could be.

Martin scowled. I am less than thirteen years younger than he, but I look even younger than that. The same genes that are keeping my mother's skin smooth at fifty-seven are being equally kind to me, and I'll never be taller than my present inadequate height.

Hayden finished the bottle. I put him up to my shoulder to burp and began patting, trying to think of what to say next.

"Martin is Regina's uncle and I'm Martin's wife, Aurora," I said cautiously. "Last night some things happened here."

"Don't tell me Craig hit Regina or nothing like that."

"Could you tell us who you are?" Martin asked, trying to sound very calm.

"Sure, man. I'm Rory Brown, Craig's buddy. We've been best friends forever."

"Then I have bad news for you... Rory."

"Craig's back in jail?"

I had to sit down. This was going to be worse than I thought.

"No," Martin said. "He's dead."

4

I'm no psychic, but Rory Brown seemed genuinely stunned by this news. He sank back down to the couch, his face contorted with horror and disbelief. "But he was alive just a few hours ago!" Rory protested, as if it took a long time to die.

"I'm sorry," I said. "He was killed last night. We found him lying on the steps to the apartment."

"Where's Regina?" Rory's voice was hoarse with, I swear, unshed tears.

"She's nowhere to be found," my husband told him. Martin was in his thinking posture, arms crossed over his chest, fingers tapping. As he reached a decision, Martin moved toward the telephone.

"You calling the police?" Rory slid onto his knees. "Man, please don't! I'm violating my parole. They'll send me back to jail for sure. I'm not even supposed to see Craig, much less leave the state with him!"

"Parole." Martin said it thoughtfully, as if parole were a common condition among his acquaintances. "You were in jail with Craig?"

"Uh, well, yeah. You know. We, uh, we wrote a few bad checks."

So Rory wasn't any desperate felon. I hadn't known how tense I was until I relaxed.

"Whose name did you sign to the bad checks?" Martin asked. I glanced at him admiringly, for making a point I'd never have considered.

"Well," Rory said, trying on his charming grin, "ours. Or it'd have been forgery. Much more serious."

Rory seemed to know his way around the penal code.

"Craig's boss would have paid him that money at the end of the month; we just needed it a little earlier than that."

Martin and I looked at each other with raised eyebrows. This sounded very weak to me. It was becoming all too clear that Regina had made a poor choice in the man she married. Of course, some people thought I had done the same when I married Martin. Ha! At least Martin had never been in jail! I *thought.* I opened my mouth to make what would have been a very ill-timed query, when we were interrupted.

The phone rang, startling all of us out of our skins. In Hayden's case, this naturally meant he started to cry. I began patting him more rapidly, saying "Sshhhh, baby," in an increasingly frantic whisper, as Martin grimaced at me while he tried to hear the caller.

"Give him his Binky," suggested Rory.

"His what?" I patted faster.

"His pacifier."

A lightbulb went on in my head as I remembered seeing Lizanne's baby sucking on a plastic thing.

"Where?" I asked eagerly. "Where is one?"

"You didn't find one in the diaper bag?"

Martin's scowl increased in ferocity.

"No." I scooted into the kitchen as fast as I could, burdened with Hayden, and returned with the diaper bag. I thrust it at Rory. "Find one!" I told him.

The young man turned the bag around, opened a Velcroed flap, and reached in a pocket, one I hadn't even noticed. He pulled out a plastic and rubber object and offered it to me.

It looked like it had lint on it. I stuck it in Hayden's mouth anyway.

Blessed silence.

Rory beamed at me angelically. Hayden's face looked just as sweet, all of a sudden. Martin became my handsome husband instead of Ebenezer Scrooge. I felt as if the vise clamping my temples had been loosened a couple of turns. I sat down on the couch very carefully, easing Hayden onto his back. He looked up at me with hazy blue eyes, relaxed and content.

"Hello, sweetie," I said softly, watching the baby's hands curl and straighten. His fingernails, his tiny fingernails, how would I ever cut them?

Martin said into the receiver, "So you haven't found her or seen any sign of the car?"

I snapped back into our current situation with some reluctance.

"Umm-hmmm," he said. "I understand."

Rory was looking down at the shabby boots on his feet, and I could practically feel the force of his hope that Martin would say nothing.

"She hasn't called here," Martin said, as if he were confirming what the caller had already stated. "No." While he was talking, Martin was eyeing Rory with the same calculation he showed when he was hiring someone. Martin seemed to reach a conclusion. He turned his back on the boy. "No, we don't know anything more than you do. Please keep us posted. Anything you find out, we want to know as soon as possible." After another minute's worth of listening, Martin hung up.

"If you don't explain things to my satisfaction," he told Rory grimly, "I'll pick up the telephone in a minute. Now, when did Regina have this baby and why didn't anyone know about it?"

"Could I have something to eat and a little trip to your bathroom before I have to explain?" Rory asked.

"You're welcome to go to the bathroom," Martin said, "but before we feed you, we have to know more about you."

The young man looked surprised at Martin's refusal. I was a little embarrassed at not offering hospitality right away, but I could see Martin's point. We'd probably already made a mistake in not calling the police the moment we'd seen him. We shouldn't compound that mistake by turning Rory into our welcome guest.

While Martin showed Rory the downstairs bathroom, I put Hayden upstairs in the portable crib and took a minute or two to get dressed. Jeans and a sweater, a vigorous tooth- and hair-brushing, and I felt like a better woman. I put on my red glasses to set off my navy sweater. After I ran a brush through my tight waves, my hair crackled with so much electricity that it flew around my head like an angry brown cloud.

This might be the only moment I had to myself today, I figured, so I called the hospital in Atlanta to ask about John.

Mother answered the phone in his room. She told me in that hushed voice people reserve for bedsides of the very ill that John was resting, that tests were ongoing, and that John had definitely had a cardiac incident, which I interpreted as "heart attack."

"What are his options?" I asked, and Mother said all those buzzwords like "angioplasty" and "stress tests." I barely listened, because all I wanted was the bottom line: Was John likely to die soon or not? After I'd gathered that he was going to live, barring some sudden and drastic circumstance, I was content to save the details of his treatment until I could spare a portion of my brain to understand what was entailed.

Mother didn't say a word about the baby. She was preoccupied, too.

I tightened the laces on my high-tops and tried to tiptoe down the stairs. Martin and Rory were in the kitchen, and I saw that Martin had relented enough to pour the boy a cup of coffee and microwave a couple of cinnamon rolls for him. Rory looked up when I entered, and let a gleam of admiration show a little too obviously. So I didn't offer to fix him any bacon or eggs.

"Rory here was just telling me about Craig," Martin said. He was sitting opposite our visitor, his arms crossed over his chest, his face relaxed and cool. Mr. Skeptical.

"What was he saying?" I slipped into a chair at one end of the table. The back part of my brain was wondering if I could borrow a baby monitor from someone. Wasn't that what the surveillance thing was called?

"I was telling Mr. Bartell, I've been Craig's friend since we were little. Our folks were friends, too. Then when

Craig's mom and dad died, Craig moved in with his aunt and uncle, Mr. and Mrs. Harbor. His brother, Dylan, was old enough to be on his own but too young to keep an eye on Craig, and the Harbors were glad to have him." Rory paused to take a bite of cinnamon roll, and I worked on keeping the relationships straight in my head.

"And that was the couple at Regina's wedding, the people who acted in the place of Craig's parents?"

"That was his aunt and uncle, Mr. and Mrs. Harbor," Rory confirmed. "They had raised four girls of their own. But now Mr. Harbor, he's kind of sickly."

Martin and I sat blinking at him like foolish owls.

"Would that be Hugh Harbor?" Martin asked, obviously dredging the name up from his distant memory.

"Yep," Rory mumbled, caught with more sweet roll in his mouth. "Mrs. Harbor used to be a Thurlkill."

"And your folks?"

"My mother, Cathy, used to be a Thurlkill, too," Rory said, seeming rather proud of the fact. "Me and Craig're kind of related. My dad is Chuck Brown, his dad was Ross Graham."

Martin looked away from the table, letting his gaze light on the front of the refrigerator. I knew he was thinking deep thoughts because his fingers were twiddling, the way they do when he's having ideas he can't talk about.

"Craig's brother was at the wedding," he said abruptly. "He seemed like a nice enough guy."

"Dylan's a great guy," Rory agreed readily. "And he and his wife, Shondra, they have the cutest little girl."

Martin did a little more staring and twiddling.

I felt like I had to say something.

"Rory, when you feel like freshening up, there's a toothbrush in a plastic wrapper in the top drawer in the downstairs bathroom," I told our surprise guest. "There are extra towels in the closet by the sink, and I think I have shampoo and soap out and ready."

Rory took the not-too-subtle hint in a jiffy. "That was real good," he told Martin sincerely, carrying his coffee cup and plate over to the sink.

I had another thought. "If you'd like to set your clothes out the bathroom door, I'll throw 'em in the washer," I offered. I rose to go upstairs to check on Hayden. "I'll put a robe in the bathroom first."

"Thank you, ma'am," he said, smiling shyly.

Martin was staring at Rory as if he were an alien wearing an ill-fitting human suit. I padded out of the room and began taking the stairs at my usual pace, and then realized I'd have to go slower. The night before had taken its toll, and toting the baby around had already made my arms trembly. I was in no shape to be thrown into the role of mother.

It wasn't any trouble finding a robe for Rory to use, since when people can't think of anything to give Martin, they give him bathrobes. Some men get gloves, some men get ties; my husband gets bathrobes. Last year, my seldom-seen father had sent us matching green terry ones (which made us look like walking bundles of Astroturf). Martin's son, Barrett, had sent him a silk paisley, and my mother had given him a blue flannel. The year before that, Barby had presented him with the nicest one of all, gray polished cotton with his monogram in maroon.

I hung the green terry robe in the downstairs bathroom and Rory scooted in. A few minutes later, his clothes were deposited discreetly outside the bathroom door, and I went to the washer and dryer closet at the rear of the house in the kitchen to start a load. There was always something in the laundry basket I could throw in with a small bundle of clothes.

Martin had gotten the portable phone and was punching in a series of numbers, peering at a page in his personal address book. He looked up at the kitchen wall clock as he listened to the ringing at the other end.

"Hello," he said. I thought he sounded uncertain, which was rare for Martin. "Cindy Bartell, please."

I began to load dishes into the dishwasher—anything to stay in the room and keep working without making it obvious I was determined to listen to this conversation.

"Cindy? This is Martin. Have you been doing well? Barrett told me you'd taken a partner on ... yes, he called me at work last week."

Barrett hated to call here because I might answer the phone.

"I'm glad you're finally getting some free time. Who'd you ... ?"

Martin's face underwent the oddest change.

"Dennis Stinson," he said. "Hmmm." He looked as if he were restraining all kinds of comments. I gathered Dennis Stinson was not unknown to Martin; but frankly, Cindy's business dealings were not my prime concern at this point in time.

I just barely heard Hayden whimper upstairs, and I cringed. I went up the stairs so fast I wished I'd had Martin clocking me. I stood by the portable crib and held my hands up in a soothing gesture, as if that would calm the baby back into sleep. I noticed that my hands were shaking, and I was saying, "Sshhhh! Sshhhh!" in a kind of frantic way. Hayden's blue-veined eyelids fluttered once more before he settled back into sleep.

Feeling as though I'd just avoided a herd of stampeding buffalo, I shambled back down the stairs and collapsed into the chair across from Martin. I slumped over the table, burying my face in my folded arms. After a moment, I felt Martin's fingers in my hair. He stroked my head the way a man absently pats a dog, but I was so tired by my unusually prolonged turn at being the strong one that I found even an offhand caress comforting.

"So, have you seen Regina lately?" Martin said into the telephone.

I could hear a tinny buzz that was Cindy's answer.

"Not in five months? Did you notice, the last time you saw her, that she'd gained some weight?"

Buzz, buzz.

"She had a baby," Martin said.

I heard a kind of shriek coming from the other end.

"Yes, really."

I raised my head to look at Martin, but he was scowling at the stove while Cindy kept talking.

"I can imagine you'd want to talk to her, but the fact is . . . she's disappeared."

Buzz.

"Well, no, I can't contact Craig to ask him where she is because Craig is here. I guess the sheriff's department here will have arranged to tell his brother and the Harbors by now. This is bad news, Cindy. Craig is dead, murdered."

Buzz, buzz.

"No, it wasn't over drugs." Martin raised his eyebrows to me, indicating that we had learned another fact about the deceased Craig. "We don't know what happened, exactly, but Regina is gone, Craig is dead, and we have the baby."

Then Martin had to tell Cindy that Barby was out of touch on a cruise, and that we didn't know what to do with Hayden.

"Yes, I guess we could," Martin said cautiously. Cindy was offering some advice, I gathered. "Yes, I guess we could do that. Well, we'll talk about it, and if we decide to come, I'll give you a call when we get there."

He hung up a moment later. "Before Rory gets out of the shower," he said, keeping his voice low, "Cindy says she had no idea Regina was pregnant, and she bets no one in Corinth knew about it. Cindy said Craig had been in jail for one or two things: possession of marijuana, bad checks, that kind of stuff. His friend Rory was almost always involved with Craig's law problems, too."

"Are we going to call the sheriff about him?" I asked, tilting my head toward the bathroom door as if Martin had a choice of subjects. We could hear the pipes groan as hot water gushed out of the shower-head. The downstairs bathroom was the noisy one.

Martin stared across the hall to the door as if it could give him an answer.

"You're really thinking about not calling the sheriff," I said, my voice full of incredulity.

"Cindy suggested we bring Hayden to Craig's aunt and uncle in Corinth, the ones who raised him," Martin said. "We might as well take Rory with us. Do you think he knows anything more than he told us?"

"I have no idea." I drew myself upright in my chair, trying not to breathe fire at the stranger sitting across from me. "But I don't think we're the best judges of that. I think we've been as kind as possible, feeding him and giving him a chance to clean up, but I think now he needs to go face the music."

"You amaze me," Martin said, with no evident amazement.

"You're giving me a surprise or two yourself," I said, with equal grimness.

"Do you think that boy has brains enough to lie?"

"Just because he's stupid and sweet doesn't mean he's good," I countered.

"But, Roe, if we turn him over, it'll make things that much worse for Regina."

"How so?" If my eyebrows could've crawled up any higher, they would have been in Maine.

"Because he knows why Craig came to Lawrenceton," Martin pointed out. "And he's the only one."

I gaped at him. I honestly tried to think that one through. Finally, I shook my head. "I'm not following you at all," I admitted.

The water had stopped in the bathroom.

"He's going to tell the police whatever puts him in the best light," Martin said. He'd also noticed the water had quit pounding through the pipes. "By his own admission, Rory's been in trouble with the law, in a minor way, for years. His dad and granddad before him have done jail time. I recognized his dad's name as soon as he told me. The Thurlkills, the mother's family, is just as bad if not worse. Rory isn't going to tell anyone anything he doesn't want to."

"So what's the profit in taking him with us?"

"He may tell us. We may be able to tell, once we get on Craig and Regina's home ground, what they were doing. Find some way through this without Regina ending up in any more trouble than she's already . . ." His voice trailed off, as he realized it would be pretty hard to find more trouble for Regina.

"Why would he tell us?"

"I can only hope he will. Now that Craig's dead, why not? We can't revoke his parole or punish him for whatever he's done. Maybe if we leave him out of this as far as the law is concerned, he'll reciprocate with information."

I could think of one word for this theory, and it wasn't a polite one.

What had happened to my incisive, figure-all-the-angles husband? He could only be this gullible because it concerned his family. Had Martin ever been foolish about me? I thought not. Did that mean he loved his sister and niece more? His son? What about his first wife? I had a moment of sheer irrational rage as I stared at Martin. Then, once again, I took a deep breath and made myself recall that he had had a terrible shock the night before, that he must in some sense feel responsible for Craig's death, that his niece was missing and might, for all we knew, be dead.

Be calm and patient, I advised myself. Calm and patient.

But I was pretty close to being clean out of calmness and patience.

I heard Hayden's little noises from upstairs, and once again I plodded up and back down, this time bringing him with me, wrapped in the only blanket Regina had brought. He was definitely awake. I sat at the table holding him, looking at the bundle in my arms.

The baby's hands fluttered, and his blue eyes were wide open. He began to make the little fussy sounds I was learning would develop into a full-blown wail. My nose told me he needed changing. And he'd want to eat after that; I was willing to put money on it. We had only one more prepared baby bottle. Where could you buy the formula? Anywhere?

"I wish we could go upstairs for a while," Martin said wistfully. But he didn't look horny. He just looked like he wanted oblivion.

"Dream on," I said, spitting out each word as though it were a hunk of poisoned apple. I tried to remember if the formula had been in powder form or concentrate. Had it been milk based? Soy? I'd have to dig the can out of the trash.

My husband was staring at me with bewilderment—if you can believe that—as I picked up Hayden and trudged into the living room to change him.

Rory was standing in the living room, the big diaper bag in his hands. I stopped short.

"Just seeing how many more diapers the little fella has," he explained. He put the bag down on the low coffee table with some reluctance, and backed away.

"How many are there?"

"What?"

"How many diapers are left in the bag?" It sounded like one of those bizarre math problems you get in the lower school grades. *If it takes Suzy ten diapers a day to keep little Marge clean, and Suzy lends Tawan three diapers and uses two, how many more diapers will she need that day?*

"Six, at least, I think," Rory said.

"Thanks." When he didn't move, I said, "Do you want to change Hayden?" I held out the baby to him.

"Oh, no!" he all but yelped, backing out of the room with great speed. "No, that's okay."

I now had all the products arranged in a line on the table, and a section of newspaper spread out to put the baby on. I managed this change with relative efficiency. All the while, watching Hayden wave around his arms and legs, hearing him fuss when his bottom was exposed to the cool air, clapping a paper towel over him quickly when he began an unexpected pee, I was wondering what Rory had been doing. When Hayden was reassembled, I looked to the left, to the wide opening to the entrance hall, and behind me to the open doors to the dining room. No one in sight.

While Hayden exercised, I undertook a real search of the diaper bag. It had, besides the big central cavity, lots and lots of pockets and pouches, zippered or Velcroed. I found two extra pacifiers; a big plastic fake key ring, which I handed to Hayden; four diapers; and a faded blue dish towel that I figured Regina had used to cover her shoulder when she burped him. I rummaged through all the little pouches until I found one I'd nearly missed, because it was on one end of the bag right under the shoulder strap clip.

I slid a finger in beside the little Velcro tab that held it shut, and broke the seal. Yep, there was something in this one. The pocket was so tight I could only insert two fingers, and I slid one behind and one in front of the object and pulled up.

"Oh no oh no oh no," I breathed, and slid what I'd extracted into Hayden's receiving blanket, which I immediately wrapped around him. I lifted him and made a beeline for the kitchen, trying to act casual.

Martin and Rory were ensconced at the table with a

map of the Southeast in front of them and more detailed maps of each state we'd pass through lying ready to hand.

Just as I was trying to think of a plausible reason to talk to Martin privately, the front doorbell rang. I started to hand the baby to my husband, realized that he would feel the bundle in the blanket, realized he might well haul it out in front of his companion. That wouldn't do at all. So I veered through the kitchen doorway to the hall, scooted back down the hall, and awkwardly opened the front door with one hand.

Ellen Lowry was waiting with a stack of blankets in her arms.

"Hey, Ellen," I said, unable to keep the surprise out of my voice.

"I'm sorry to intrude, but I heard you had troubles, and I thought you could maybe use these," she said, nodding at the stack. "These are baby blankets I used when the boys were little, and I believe they're in perfect shape. I ran them through the washer and dryer this morning to freshen them up."

"How kind of you! Please, come in," I said, trying to summon some poise. I stood aside and ushered Ellen into the living room, where the square low table was covered with changing paraphernalia. Ellen smiled in a nostalgic sort of way.

"You'd think it had been so long I would've forgotten about changing the boys, but to me it seems like yesterday," she said, shaking her head in disbelief.

I forced myself to respond. This was a very gracious gesture of Ellen's, and I needed to be gracious in return. I asked if she needed something to drink, or eat; she refused. I urged her strongly to sit down and stay a while; she said she only had a minute, and sat on the edge of a rather uncomfortable chair. She asked about John's heart and the health of the baby, and ran her fingertip over Hayden's soft cheek. I was afraid she'd offer to hold him. How could I explain a refusal? But the money in the blanket would be obvious to anyone who held the baby.

Luckily, Ellen stood after a brief conversation and began her good-byes. The weak winter sun streamed through the window to make her smooth blond hair glow like a halo as she bent over me and the baby to coo at him before she picked up her purse. Ellen looked like a model in a catalog for mature women.

She was elegant, thoughtful, intelligent, and kind: and I could hardly wait for her to be gone.

Finally I could watch her car go slowly down the driveway to the road. I whipped around and strode into the kitchen, as much as you can whip and stride with a baby in your arms. Martin and Rory were sitting at the table, having an earnest conversation. I abandoned any idea I'd had of concealing my discovery.

"Do you want to tell me about this?" I said, pulling the sheaf of bills from Hayden's blanket and tossing them on top of the map.

Rory looked as though I'd slapped him.

"I didn't have anything to do with that," he said, as if he were sure I'd believe him, as if we were lifelong friends.

Martin's eyes closed, slowly. He opened them, sighed, picked up the sheaf of bills. He counted it silently. "Five hundred," he informed us.

Rory's eyes had never left the money. His face altered when Martin told us the total. I could swear I glimpsed naked rage on his face. But it softened immediately into a mask of puzzlement and anxiety.

"Would you like to tell me about this?" Martin asked him.

"That must be the money Craig stole," his best friend said hesitantly. Then Rory fell silent, his eyes fixed on the money.

If there'd been a jug of water handy I'd have thrown it on him.

"Would you care to explain a little further?" Martin's voice was deceptively mild.

Rory looked pretty darn reluctant to start explaining, but we were both waiting and I think he knew we would not change the subject.

"When Regina was expecting," Rory began, "Craig began thinking of all the things the baby was gonna need, and I guess he just kinda went crazy, since he couldn't get them for her, so he robbed a convenience store."

"In Corinth?" Martin asked.

I sat down with my burden to listen to this latest fairy tale. Hayden wasn't interested. He made little smacking noises. I looked down to discover he was asleep, with his tiny fist jammed into his mouth. I eased him into his infant seat to give my arms a rest.

"No, sir," said Rory. "He went across the state line into Pennsylvania somewhere. I don't know the exact town."

For an appreciable length of time we just sat staring at Rory, who ducked his head and blushed at our critical scrutiny. I eyed the telephone, tempted once again to pick it up and call the sheriff to come get this fool.

But Martin shook his head, reading my thoughts.

"You were out of jail when Regina had the baby?" I asked.

Rory looked as though a lightbulb were appearing over his head.

"No, ma'am. I was in the jail."

"Was Craig in jail when Regina had the baby?"

"No, ma'am. Craig got out a few days before I did."

"But Craig was back in jail for the past . . . ?"

"Well, we got picked up again two weeks ago. About."

I now understood why the police beat people who wouldn't confess. I knew somewhere in that cute, empty head lay the truth. And I wanted it badly enough to extract it with red-hot pincers, or at least so I told myself. I could tell by the way Martin was clenching his hands that he felt the same way, and I was willing to bet that under other circumstances Martin could make Rory talk.

"We'll have to talk about this more, later," I told them both.

I've never been trained to be a detective of any kind, but I'm a reasonably observant person, and this money was not the jumble of rumpled bills of all denominations you'd get if you robbed a convenience store. This was the kind of money you'd get at a bank, two one-hundred-dollar bills, the rest in twenties: a compact little bundle, smooth and flat.

5

Lunch that day was a real tense meal. I heated up soup and made grilled-cheese sandwiches, and we sat together at the kitchen table in uneasy silence. For once in my life, I wanted the phone to ring. Maybe the highway patrol would stop Regina's car. Martin had asked Cindy to try to discover the name of the cruise line with which Barby had sailed, and getting Barby here would be a great relief. Or my mother might tell me more about John's prognosis. I had so much to worry about, my thoughts were running around inside my head like hamsters.

Just as I began the dishes, I heard Hayden stirring, and this time he woke up ready to raise the roof.

I put a bottle in the microwave before I left the kitchen. I was getting numb from the unaccustomed responsibility for this baby. I had never been so tired in my life, and every time I heard him tune up to cry, I leaped into action to stave off any more wailing. My stomach clenched every time he made a noise.

An hour later, I had changed Hayden, fed Hayden, burped Hayden—in short, fulfilled my part of the bargain. But he wouldn't go back to sleep. In my opinion, he should be out of the picture until the next feeding-changing-burping cycle; but it was one he didn't seem to share. Not knowing what else to do, I was holding the baby, sitting on the couch in the library, staring down at the round face with more than a little frustration. Furthermore, I had an awful feeling that the half-done dishes were still sitting on the counter in the kitchen.

"Listen, you need to give me a break," I said. "Don't you know I only have so many interior resources?" I definitely felt the cupboard was pretty bare in my interior resources closet.

Hayden regarded me wonderingly. He didn't seem to be concerned that he was at the mercy of a totally inadequate caregiver. His arms waved around. He made little noises, "eh" and a kind of creaky grunt being the most popular. With my free finger I touched the round cheek. It was so soft. Through his thin down of fair hair, I could see the pulsing place on the top of his head where his skull had not yet joined, or so Lizanne had explained it to me. It made this small life seem incredibly vulnerable.

I had a sudden, strange impulse: I would call my friend and priest, Aubrey Scott, and have him baptize Hayden.

If my hands had been free, I'd have slapped myself after I ran that idea through my head a second time. Baptism wouldn't put a protective candy coating on Hayden. He wasn't an M&M. And to assume the responsibility of having this child baptized would indicate I had given up on Regina bobbing to the surface to reclaim him, a terrible admission.

But I knew I would've felt a lot better if I could have just eased into the church and sort of casually had Aubrey sprinkle some water over this kid. I figured that Hayden

Graham, son of Craig and Regina—if that was indeed who this child was—needed all the help he could get.

Confident that no one could hear me, I whispered, "You is booful baby." Hayden's hazy blue eyes focused on me. He smiled. My heart pounded suddenly, as if I'd just fallen in love. I beamed back at him as exaggeratedly as a children's TV show host.

Sally Allison said, "Your lips are gonna fall off if you keep that up."

I jumped. "Why'd you go and scare me like that, Sally? Good golly Miss Molly! You about made me jump out of my skin!"

"Sorry. You and Tiny Tim here just looked so cute." Sally bent over to get a close look at my lapful.

"You heard about our predicament, I guess."

"Mild-mannered reporter Sally Allison sees all, tells most."

"Got any news?" Having had her look, Sally threw herself in Martin's luxurious chair while my blood pressure finally settled back down to normal.

"Hmmm. Well, police found Regina's car."

"What?"

"You heard me." Sally was carefully patting her right hand against her bronze curls, a gentle sort of pat that wouldn't disarrange the perfect arc they formed around her head. She was checking for holes. Next, she'd pull her compact out of her purse and powder her nose; then she'd rummage for a lipstick and redefine her mouth. This was Sally's personal checklist. As she opened her compact, she said, "It was just across the state line in South Carolina."

"Any sign of Regina?"

Sally shook her head. "No, honey, I'm sorry. But on the big plus side, no bloodstains." Sally carefully crossed her legs, smoothing the skirt of her expensive green suit.

Hayden smiled at me again, and it dawned on me that he didn't smell very good. In fact, that was putting it nicely.

"I can't imagine what happened," I said absently, wriggling forward on the couch so I could stand with the baby. I managed this, and took him to the living room, which I'd definitely settled on as the best place to keep the diaper bag and the rubberized pad that you put under Hayden before you took off his diaper. (Experience had taught me the use of the pad.) With scarcely a fumble and no missed snaps, I wiped Hayden's bottom and changed him. I dropped the soiled wipes in the dirty diaper before I rolled it up and retaped it shut, a refinement of which I was extremely proud.

"Good job," Sally said approvingly, taking the used diaper from me and marching through the dining room to dispose of it in the kitchen. I heard the gush of running water as she washed her hands.

"I take it Martin knows about the car?" I called.

Sally gave me a funny look. I caught the tail end of it as she rejoined me in the living room. "Yes, the sheriff came to tell him. They're out there talking in the yard."

In the yard. Why would Martin talk to the sheriff outside? It was cold, and windy, and ... oh shit. Where was our unwanted houseguest? That was why Martin was keeping the sheriff outside.

"What's wrong?" Sally was paying attention, as usual.

"Nothing!" I said brightly. I was darting little looks out to the hall, the dining room, the kitchen, to see if I could spy Rory. When I looked back at Sally, she was looking skeptical, to say the least.

"And you say," she began, her voice an extension of that skeptical look, "that you have no idea what happened out here? Excuse me, Roe, but that's hardly like you."

"Listen here, Sally Allison, I have a lapful of trouble without you adding to it," I said, to my own surprise. Then I burst into tears. If I'd been able to choose, I could hardly have picked a more effective diversion. While Hayden lay on his back on the coffee table, looking around him with increasingly heavy eyes, Sally patted my shoulder vigorously.

I found myself Telling Sally All About It, which means I was telling her my singular emotional reaction to the whole day yesterday, culminating with the appearance of my mother in the kitchen this morning with her own terrible news.

Sally's pats gradually grew less and less emphatic and more and more punitive.

"What?" I asked, when it dawned on me that she looked sour rather than sympathetic.

"Not about you, is it?" she asked brusquely.

"What?"

"All this. Your stepfather's sick, so your mother is preoccupied with him, as she should be. Your husband's niece is missing and her husband is dead, so Martin's thinking more about his family than he is about you, for once."

I stared at Sally like a landed fish. Was I really that selfish? Or had Sally been so jealous of me all these years, and I hadn't noticed? I felt like I'd been negotiating a minefield and the soldier behind me had started chucking rocks over my shoulder.

"You know, Sally, this maybe isn't the best time to tell me about my character flaws," I said in as even a voice as I could manage. "I had in mind something like you telling me, 'There, there, you poor thing,' rather than implying I'm a selfish bitch who thinks I'm the center of the universe."

Of course, no matter what I said, I was wondering how much of what Sally had said was true. Did everyone see me that way? Oh God, had all the friends I'd had all these years looked at me and thought, That Roe, she's okay, but talk about egocentric!

Sally looked stricken, thank God. But my relief faded when she said, "Roe, my timing stinks, I apologize for that. But you've never known how lucky you've had it. Your mother does everything but wipe your rear for you, and your husband not only thinks he should protect and pamper you, but he has money!"

"And that's my fault?"

"No!" she said. "No! But it's your—responsibility!" She looked at her watch and gasped. "City council meeting! I have to go now, Roe, I'll see you soon." And she grabbed her purse and flew out the door before I had a chance to respond.

I scooped up the sleeping Precious Burden and watched through the window as Sally crossed the yard, pausing to talk to Martin and the sheriff. I was glad to see Martin was wearing his waterproof jacket, since the day was overcast and every now and then the sky spit some rain. The sheriff strolled away from Martin and leaned on Sally's car, talking to her through the partly open window for a moment before Sally gave a quick wave and swung her car around.

I picked and puzzled at the scene with Sally, which had

upset me deeply. I felt like I hadn't known the lion was within when I'd shut the village gates for the night. Gee whiz—Roe Teagarden, Monster of Selfishness?

I'd always thought of myself more as Roe Teagarden, the Incredibly Lucky. Well... sometimes. Maybe not a few years ago, when my steady boyfriend had suddenly married the woman he'd gotten pregnant while he was dating me... but then again, I'd been lucky I hadn't married him, right? And maybe I hadn't been so lucky when my father and stepmother had moved my half brother out of state, making it almost impossible for me to see him... but then again, I'd saved his life, and I'd gotten to fly out to California to visit Phillip twice since then.

This "good luck" evaluation was just as helpful as opening the closet full of bridesmaids' dresses I'd kept in my storage closet before I'd met Martin. Time to shuffle off this coil of introspection and deal with a here-and-now situation.

Hayden was asleep. His eyelids were so pale the veins stood out clearly, making his skin look almost translucent. I lowered my head to inhale his scent.

"I cheated you," Martin said. He was standing in the archway to the dining room. He hadn't shaved, and his hair was rumpled. The stubble on his cheeks was white, like his hair, not black, like his eyebrows.

I wasn't in the mood for any more deep emotional scenes.

"How do you figure that?" I asked, my voice hushed and level because of the baby.

"We could have explored other options," he said, his voice equally subdued. "Maybe your"—he nodded toward my midsection to indicate my malformed womb—"could have been corrected surgically or something. We could have adopted privately; we have enough money."

I looked at my husband for a long, wake-up moment before I said, "And these are new thoughts to you?"

I carried Hayden up the stairs and laid him in his crib.

Then I marched downstairs. Martin was standing right where I'd left him. I said, "I shouldn't hop on you with both feet because something was more important to me than it was to you."

It was like my words didn't register, as if Martin had become deaf to anything that didn't resonate with some mysterious preoccupation. "We should start out tomorrow morning," he said. "We'll have to drive. Given the circumstances. Maybe you should go to the store and get whatever the baby will need for the trip."

Like I knew? I opened my mouth to protest, then shut it again. Sally's observation had stung me where it hurt, had made me doubt my every impulse. I went to the desk to make a list of things I might need, but instead I sat with my hand on the telephone. Despite a nagging fear that somehow this conversation, too, would be dispiriting, I called the one person I could count on, my best friend, Amina.

Wife of a Houston lawyer, Amina was the mother (and I the godmother) of a lovely little girl, Megan. Amina, an only child, and her husband, oldest of two siblings, were happily indulging Megan (now a Terrible Two) and threatening her with a brother or sister.

"Amina," I said, relief throbbing through my voice when my friend answered the phone.

"Roe," she said, in a curiously hushed voice. "I can't talk long, Megan's got the measles."

Of course.

"Is she very sick?" I asked, trying to sound Deeply Concerned.

"Just the usual case, I guess." Amina was trying to be brave, not doing a very good job of it. "But she just needs me every minute, or at least she thinks she does. I've been taking her Popsicles and playing games with her all day. Do you think she's a little spoiled? That's what Hugh's mom says."

"Only as much as any only child," I told Amina, somewhat grimly. I had grown up as an only child.

"We'll take care of that soon," Amina said, with the confidence that comes of getting pregnant on your honeymoon. "Thank God I'm not pregnant now, since I have to take care of her and measles are so scary if you're expecting. Oh hell, I hear her calling. Again."

I cocked an eyebrow. Amina was wearing a little thin in the nursing department. I wasn't surprised. Tall, energetic, and attractive, Amina had always been a person who had to keep moving, had always had a project in the wings and another to keep her currently occupied.

"I'll let you go in just a minute," I promised, "but I need some information first."

"What can I help you with?" Amina's voice had fallen even lower.

"What supplies do you need to take care of an infant for maybe two or three days?"

After a moment's thoughtful silence, Amina began, "Four sleepers, about twenty diapers . . ." I wrote furiously on the notepad I kept by the phone. Bless Amina, she didn't ask any questions. If I wasn't going to get to cry on her shoulder, I might as well not go through the whole explanation.

After I hung up and checked on Hayden, I found my coat slung over a chair in the dining room. I put it on and grabbed my purse. Martin and Rory had a football game on in the den. I didn't think either of them could have told me the score if I'd asked, but I wouldn't have put money on it. To make sure I had their attention, I stood in front of the screen.

"Martin," I said, hoping I didn't sound like a total shrew, "the dishes are still on the counter from lunch. Please do them by the time I come back. Rory, you listen for the baby. He's asleep upstairs." They both stared at me groggily, so I didn't move until I had confirming nods from both of them.

It was a real pleasure to leave the house.

I turned a country music station up real loud as I drove to that new southern cultural center, Wal-Mart. Somehow, country music seemed to fit the low-down strangeness of the past two days. "My Husband's Niece Done Hacked Her Man"—how would that play? Or "Whose Baby Am I Feeding?" Nah, couldn't think of a chorus for that one. What about "There's a Dead Man on My Stairs and a Baby 'Neath the Bed"?

That kept me smiling until I got past the greeter (who happened to be a cousin of my husband's secretary and always had to pass the time of day with me due to that connection), got my cart (known locally as a "buggy"), and set off down the main aisle. I wheeled my buggy toward a corner I seldom visited, the corner full of baby paraphernalia. I had my little list with me, the list I'd scribbled while I was on the phone with Amina, and I studied it with care. I bought: a package of Pampers, a can of powdered formula, some baby bottles, three more sleepers in what I estimated was Hayden's weight range, one rubberized bib, another baby blanket, an extra set of fake keys, and four spare Binkys. I thought pacifiers were the most wonderful inventions on earth, and I planned to boil them and put them in little plastic bags and stow one in my purse, my coat, and Martin's coat, and keep the spare in the diaper bag.

I paused, my hand resting on a box of wet wipes. I looked down at the fuzzy sleepers in the buggy. Why did Hayden need clothes? I put the wet wipes in the buggy very slowly, wondering. I recalled the look of the apartment, the open suitcase, the spill of clothes.

Clothes for Regina. Not clothes for the baby.

Aimlessly, I began pushing the buggy around the store, trying to figure out what that meant. Regina had known she was going on a trip. But she hadn't planned on taking Hayden? Or—she hadn't had a baby when she started on the trip? That didn't make any sense.

Shaking my head, I realized I'd plowed into men's wear. I slipped a pair of jeans and a flannel shirt into the cart. They were smaller than Martin's usual, but I hoped no one would think of noticing. Probably Rory also needed underwear, but I'd be damned if I'd pick it out. I tucked the "no clothes for Hayden" thought into a side pocket of my mind, to pull out and reexamine later.

While I was in the men's section, I was lucky enough to run into our closest neighbor, Clement Farmer. He was staring dubiously at a rack of silk boxer shorts. Clement was a small man, almost bald, with a few wisps of white hair over his ears. He had a red complexion and very white even teeth, which made him look overall like a Christmas elf.

"I told Padgett I saw a car pulling out of your drive the other night," Clement said, without any preliminaries.

"Is that so?"

"Yes, it was a dark red car with Ohio plates."

Regina's car.

"Who was in it?" I asked, dreading the answer.

"Two people. I couldn't see the driver very well, but the passenger was a dark-haired young woman."

Sounded like Regina.

I was in more of a hurry than ever to get home and tell Martin. I thanked Clement for telling me (though I wondered why he hadn't called us on the phone) and asked him to feed Madeleine for us while we were gone. She hated to be checked into the vet's almost as much as the vet's staff hated to see her coming.

"Sure!" Clement agreed, obviously pleased. He was the only person I'd ever met who seemed to genuinely like Madeleine. "Think she'll need a brushing?"

"Oh, I'm sure it wouldn't hurt." I'd made one person happy today, anyway.

I loaded my purchases into Martin's Mercedes and stopped by the filling station to top up the tank. Home again, this time to find the dishes done and in the drainer; Rory watching television in our den (still, or again); and Hayden continuing his nap. Martin was packing in his usual efficient pattern, and I noticed he'd gotten out his extreme-cold-weather gear, which he seldom needed in Lawrenceton.

It seemed grossly unfair that Hayden slept when he was alone with Martin.

I told Martin what Clement Farmer had seen the night before.

"So she's a hostage, if it was Regina Clement saw," he said.

"Could be, Martin." I wondered how he'd gotten that out of the story I'd told him, but shook my head and decided not to pursue it. I thought of sharing my wonderment about the lack of provision for Hayden with Martin, but he looked so distracted I decided I'd be wasting my breath. I turned and went downstairs.

I sat at the kitchen table studying the directions on the can of formula powder. I read them over and over, determined not to do Hayden harm with my ignorance. I assembled everything I'd need, down to the same pan I remembered Regina using. I had a hard time believing I'd talked to Regina while she prepared formula right here in this kitchen, less than twenty-four hours before.

While I waited for the water to boil, I called John's hospital again, talked to my mother once more, found out John was out of the room having a test.

Our telephone persisted in its curious silence. I did get a call or two from older friends of my mother's, asking about John; but other than our priest, Aubrey, no one seemed to want to know how Martin and I were handling our own little corner of Craig's tragedy. I wondered forlornly at that, but then I decided that no one knew quite what to say.

A brusque rap at the back door made me look up sharply while I was sealing bottles of formula to put in the refrigerator. I'd made enough to last us the trip to Ohio, I estimated, having no idea what I'd do if I'd figured wrong. Could you buy formula ready to serve? I hadn't remembered to check while I was at the store. I was so lost in worries about feeding Hayden that it took me a second to realize I was happy to see my friend and former employee Angel Youngblood and to translate that happiness into a smile.

Only the fact that Angel was preceded by a huge bulge kept me from hugging her, which would have surprised both of us. Angel is almost a foot taller than me, and golden and rangy as a leopard. Though now she looked like a really pregnant leopard, the effect was still striking. I couldn't remember exactly how old Angel was, but I was sure she was at least six years younger than I, and her husband, Shelby, was a few months older than Martin. Shelby and Martin had been buddies in Vietnam, and had met sporadically after the war and their covert activities in South America had concluded. Now Shelby worked for Martin as a crew leader at the Pan-Am Agra plant.

"Where's the baby?" Angel was always direct. I called up the stairs softly, to alert Martin, and led Angel up to have a look. Martin, who'd been reading a magazine (or at least staring at its open pages), rose when Angel came in, seemed to pull himself together a little. Angel just nodded at him. She was absorbed in the tiny face. She put her long fingers around the curve of Hayden's skull, and she laid her other hand on the mound of her pregnancy. The mound constricted—that's the best way I can describe it—and, after a long moment, relaxed.

Angel smiled at me. "This one doesn't even have room to move around anymore," she said, her voice quiet and smooth so as not to wake Hayden.

"Isn't it almost time for you?"

Angel nodded. "Time, and a day over. But I'm feeling fine, so today's not the day, I guess. I'm sorry about your stepfather," she added, jumping mentally from her own hospital stay to John's. "How's he doing? How's your mother holding up?"

My mother and Angel had developed an arm's-length mutual respect.

"She's doing pretty well." You know my mother, my voice said.

Angel nodded, her eyes back on the baby's face. "There's something about them," she said, the smooth low voice almost hypnotic. "You'd kill for them." Her hands caressed her own stomach again, and I saw it tighten again.

"If they're your own," I said, a question in my tone.

"Maybe not just then. Look at him." And Angel crouched over the pale-green-and-blue portable crib, her blond hair framing her narrow face.

"What are you gonna do with him, Roe? If I understand right, his dad is dead and his mother is missing," Angel said, as we went back downstairs to the kitchen. She sat at the table while I poured her a glass of orange juice.

"We're planning on driving to Corinth, where Regina and her husband were living," I explained. "Then, I guess we'll see if Craig's family will keep him. Or maybe Regina will have turned up by then, and we'll know what happened. Or ... we'll be able to get in touch with Barby, and when she flies back from her cruise, she'll be coming into Pittsburgh, which is the closest airport to Corinth."

It sounded pretty thin and uncertain, even to me.

"Wouldn't it be better to stay put?" Angel drank her juice in one long gulp and set the glass down. She eased forward in her chair, and her hand rubbed her back absently. Her face tightened suddenly, then relaxed. "After all," Angel said slowly, with effort, "if Regina does escape, or return ..."

Her face did that tightening and relaxing thing again. "She'd come back here, for her baby..." This time Angel's face stayed tight for a while.

"Angel?"

"I think," she said slowly and thoughtfully, "that maybe it will be today, after all."

I was on my feet in a flash. I'd seen one baby born, and I wasn't about to do that again. "Let me drive you to the hospital," I said. "I'll get my jacket."

"No, that would get the cars all confused," Angel said, but as if she hardly knew what she was saying. All her attention seemed to be focused inward. "My car would be out here, and who knows when I could come back to get it. I can drive home, and wait there for Shelby to get off work."

"Call him from here."

"Okay," she said, to my surprise. My concern deepened. Easy capitulation was not one of Angel's characteristics. "Let me use the bathroom first."

I hovered outside the door.

When Angel emerged, she said, "Today for sure." Her voice was still calm and flat, but I sensed all kinds of suppressed excitement just trying to bubble to the surface. She went to the telephone on the kitchen wall, walking in a kind of tentative way, as if she expected something to grab her at every step. I bounced around her like a rubber ball, anxious to help, trying not to get in the way, scared to death she'd have the baby here.

Angel punched Shelby's work number, waited for an answer, all the while that inner-directed look on her face.

I heard a squawk from the other end of the line.

"Jason Arlington, that you? This is Angel. I need to talk to Shelby," Angel said.

I could hear the tiny voice squawk some more.

"Yes, you can sound the siren," Angel said, sounding as if she were holding on to her patience by a very taut leash. The siren's wail was audible from where I was standing.

"Shelby's crew think it's real funny that he's going to be a father for the first time," Angel explained. "They set up this siren to call him if he's far out in the plant when I phone to tell him the baby's on the way." Her face tightened again, and her fingers clenched the receiver until they turned white. Then, gradually, she relaxed. She smiled into the telephone. Her husband was on the other end.

"Shelby," Angel said. "I'm going to leave right now to drive back into town. I'm at Martin and Roe's. Meet me at our house."

This time I could hear Shelby's words. "You stay right there," he bellowed. "I'll come get you. Don't you try to drive!"

To my amazement, Angel said, "All right."

I think Shelby was startled, too, because there was silence on the other end of the line. Then he said, "I'll be right there," and the line went dead.

I caught a glimpse of Rory Brown stepping quietly down the hall. Angel's back was turned, and frankly I don't think she'd have cared if a real leopard went through the house, at that point.

I went to the foot of the stairs and called Martin, who came down with a newly awake Hayden. Martin tried not to look dismayed when I explained the situation. He handed me the baby immediately.

Angel seemed to want to remain standing, so I tried not to fuss over her. I put a bottle in the microwave, and Angel said, "That's not a safe way to heat bottles."

"What?"

"Sometimes they have hot spots if you heat them that way. That's what the baby book said."

Everyone's a critic. "So far, we haven't had any problem," I said. "I'm testing it before I give it to him."

Angel shrugged, as if she'd done her best and it wasn't her fault if I was misguided. I shook the bottle vigorously, tested the formula on my arm, and sat down to feed Hayden, who had just let out a few preliminary "eh" noises.

Angel did the face-clenching routine again. This time she propped herself against the wall.

"Are they getting worse?" I asked, while Martin looked as if he wished he were on the moon.

"Maybe I should call the ambulance," he suggested.

I noticed he didn't suggest taking Angel into town himself. I had a sneaking suspicion he was worried Angel's water would break in his Mercedes.

"No," she said, shaking her head. Martin tried not to look relieved. "I know this is going to take hours. I'm just trying to get used to the feeling. It's like a clamp. Then there's the release. Then, along after a while comes the next clamp."

"Does it hurt?"

"Not yet, but it's on a roll downhill," Angel said. "I hope Shelby doesn't pass out in the labor room. He got sick when I broke my leg a few years ago."

A battered car sped up our driveway, and Shelby, tall and pockmarked and burly with muscle, was out of the vehicle and in our kitchen door before you could say "Having a baby." His dark hair, liberally streaked with gray, was dented all around where his hard hat had rested, and his Fu Manchu mustache was going in all directions, as if he'd rubbed his hands over it.

Wordlessly, Shelby shook hands with Martin, kissed me on the forehead with nary a glance at the baby I was holding, and took his wife by the elbow to hustle her out the door. Angel gave us a nod and they were on their way, Shelby shepherding Angel as though she were the only woman who'd ever given birth. "Jason said he'd get one of the guys to drive him out here to pick up Angel's car; I gave him a spare key," Shelby called over his shoulder at the last minute. Then he buckled up and headed back into town to the Lawrenceton hospital.

Rory came out of the den when Shelby had turned out of the driveway. He was looking amused.

"So, she's gonna have a baby really soon," he said agreeably. Listening at doors did not seem to present a moral dilemma for Rory Brown. "Craig took Regina to a midwife." Then the reminiscent smile faded from the boy's face as he remembered that his friend Craig was now dead. "He told me it was a lot cheaper," Rory added, with no smile at all.

"I have to pack," I said, and both the men looked at me.

"Okay," Rory said, after what I could only think of as a pregnant pause, "I'll feed the little fella."

I transferred baby and bottle to the young man, and spent a blessed hour alone upstairs, trying to assemble clothes suitable for an Ohio winter. A number of important questions bobbed to the surface of my mind as I folded and figured. Where would we stay in Corinth? The Holiday Inn I'd used before would certainly be cramped with a baby sharing the room. I wondered about the farmhouse Martin owned up there, the one in which he'd grown up. He'd had it restored from its near-derelict condition, he'd mentioned in passing.

"We could stay in the farmhouse," Martin said from the doorway, and I jumped in my skin. "I didn't mean to scare you," he said.

"I was just thinking about the farmhouse," I said, when my heart had stopped trying to make tracks out of my chest. "You had it repaired?"

"Yes... and to confess something to you, Regina and Craig were living in it."

"Why should you say 'confess'?" I asked. I sat down on the end of the bed, two unopened packages of panty hose in my hands.

"I didn't tell you," he said. He wandered across the room to stand looking out the window. His shoulders had an uncharacteristic slump. The bleak view of winter fields couldn't have helped his state of mind much. It was a gray day, and the clouds were full of rain... Pregnant with it, in fact, my brain told me chirpily. I dropped the hose on the floor and clutched my head with both hands.

"Why didn't you tell me, Martin? Why did that have to be such a big secret?"

He sat beside me on the foot of the bed. He put one arm around me, carefully, as though he realized there was a good chance I'd sock him in the nose.

"Cindy told me you would always keep secrets," I said. "She said you couldn't help it." I'd never told Martin about the conversation I'd had with his first wife before Martin and I were married. I'd been convinced he'd learned his lesson during his first marriage, that with me he would not repeat the same mistake.

"I've never lied to you about anything," Martin said now, and that was something else Cindy had told me.

I *hated* her being right.

"Martin, if there's something you know about this that you haven't told me, if there's anything about Craig and Regina and Rory and Cindy or your sister… *anything* you haven't told me, this is your last free pass."

"After this I get penalized?" His face fell into more familiar lines, the uncertainty fading to be replaced with the intelligence and command he normally wore like his suit coat.

"After this, you get thrown out of the game." I looked him straight in his pale brown eyes.

"But I'm still in?"

I nodded.

His mouth only had to move an inch to cover mine.

It was different, this time; we'd always been perfect together in bed, and this morning he still had the magic to make me lost in the act of love; but now he was rougher, more demanding. It was as if he were reasserting his exclusive right to me, daring some cosmic force to just try to separate us. You woman, me man, his body said, and mine gasped, Hoo boy.

6

We started out in the dark early the next morning. We didn't want anyone to see Rory in the car with us. He was sitting in back with the baby for now, though I planned on switching seats with him later, at least for a little while. Martin would do the driving: He much preferred to be in the driver's seat. What a shock, right?

We didn't even go through a drive-through to get coffee until we'd been on the road an hour. Rory was asleep, and after a sip or two I woke up enough to want to talk to Martin.

"What did you do about Shelby and Angel?" he asked.

"I left a message on the answering machine at Buds 'N Blooms," I said. I inhaled the coffee vapor. "They'll take her a huge pink bouquet today." Shelby had called at midnight to tell us that Angel had had a baby girl, a seven-pounder. He had been exhausted and elated; I could never have imagined hearing Shelby sound so *grateful.*

"Gift?" Martin asked tentatively, aware he was on shaky ground here.

"I gave her a baby shower," I reminded him, noticing a warning edge in my voice. "Mother and I gave her a playpen."

"And how is John?"

"Mother called at ten last night to tell me John would be in the hospital for a day or two more. The doctors are sure he had a heart attack, and they're still talking about treatment options."

"How's he feeling?"

"Scared."

"And Aida?"

"She's scared, too, but you would find it hard to tell."

Martin was closer to my mother's age than mine, but it still felt strange to hear him call her by her first name.

"I know how hard this is on you." In the lightening gloom, I could tell Martin had turned briefly to look at me, before refocusing on the highway. "I expected you to tell me any minute to take Hayden back up to Ohio myself, that you were staying with your mother."

"Martin," I said, "it never occurred to me to do that."

We rode in silence for at least half an hour after that.

A long car trip in the winter with a baby . . . when you've never had a baby . . . the formula for disaster, right?

The best I can say is, it could've been worse. For example, someone could have pulled out my eyelashes one by one.

We stopped to feed and change the baby . . . well, we stopped so I could feed and change the baby. Oddly enough, it wasn't the physical work of caring for Hayden that was so exhausting, though that was tough, too. What was most difficult was an unexpected aspect of traveling with a child: the observations of strangers. I hadn't realized every mother learns to discuss her child with every waitress; restroom customer; and Tom, Dick, and Harry who walks by. The restaurant where we stopped for lunch gave me my first sampling. I carried Hayden in his infant seat, found it was impossible to fit it anywhere on the table or on one chair, and finally discovered that if Martin and Rory sat on one side of a booth, I could put the infant seat and myself on the other side. This did not make Martin happy, but at that point, making Martin happy was low on my priority list.

The waitress, a plump black woman with gorgeous up-slanted eyes, gave me my first taste of what was to come. "Oh, he so cute!" she said, with apparent sincerity. "How old is he?"

"A month," I said, as Rory said, "Two and a half weeks."

She laughed as Rory and I glared at each other. "He a big baby," she said admiringly. "How much was he?"

I stared at her blankly. Cost-wise?

"He weighed eight pounds, five ounces," Rory said firmly.

So the correct answer was his birth weight. I'd try to remember that. I smiled at Rory.

"Oh, that's sweet," the woman ("Candra" her name tag read) commented, handing us menus. "The daddy knows the birth weight!"

"Oh, he's a great father," I assured her, suddenly feeling quite giddy. "He was there the whole time."

As Candra absorbed the age difference between me and Rory, her eyes widened. "Can I get you something to drink?" she asked in a subdued voice.

When we'd all ordered, I fished a bottle out of the cooler and asked Candra if she'd heat it up for us. That was another thing I learned on that trip: how to ask favors, some of them outrageous, of complete strangers. When you're functioning as a mom you have to. Would you heat this bottle? Bring extra napkins? Throw away this dirty diaper? Pretend not to hear my child screaming his head off?

My most humiliating moment came in Kentucky at a rest stop, when I carried Hayden into the ladies' room to change his diaper. I had the baby, the diaper bag, and my purse. I changed him somehow—at least that particular freezing rest room had a foldout tray to do the job on—but then I found I had to use the facilities myself quite urgently, and I had nowhere to put him and no time to carry him out to Martin. I don't think I've done anything as complicated in my life as try to pull down my slacks and underwear in a cubicle the size of a phone booth while holding a baby, a bulky diaper bag, and a purse, and wearing a coat.

It was humiliating. And though it probably would've made *America's Funniest Home Videos,* at the time it wasn't at all amusing to me. As a matter of fact, as I began wearily to reverse the process, I decided I'd *never* think it was funny.

And I knew for a fact that Martin would never get over being called "Grandpa" by one well-meaning cashier. It was lucky for Rory that Martin hadn't noticed his suppressed smile, and lucky for me that my own face was too tired to form the grin I felt rising to my lips.

Most of our conversation on this trip consisted of Martin trying to get Rory to give us more specifics about Craig and the baby, Regina and the baby, the baby's birth, why Regina had driven down to Lawrenceton without Craig.

"Oh, well, she didn't expect us to get out of jail when

we did," Rory explained, when he saw he couldn't get away with waffling anymore. "I expect she just wanted to show off the baby to you, since her mom is out of the country."

"Does my sister know she's a grandmother?"

"Huh?"

"Does Regina's mother know Regina has had a baby?"

"Well, not to say so. Not really."

Rory was sitting in front with Martin now, and I was buckled in the back with Hayden, whom I was amusing by dangling a toy for him to focus on. I considered flattening the receiving blanket that lay in my lap, twirling the ends until it formed a long rope, then looping it around Rory's narrow neck. He'd spit out the truth then! I told myself truculently, realizing I was somewhere beyond tired.

"Is this baby really Regina's?" I asked sharply. "Or did she steal Hayden from someone?"

Martin closed his eyes briefly, then refocused on the road.

"Of course this baby is Regina's!" our companion said, as indignant as he could manage to be.

"How do you know?"

"Craig drove her to the midwife's!"

"And you watched the baby being born?"

"Hell, no!"

"But you were at the midwife's?"

"Well ..." Rory seemed to be thinking deeply, and that seemed to be difficult for him. "Not exactly, not me so much as Craig. I think I was in jail."

I looped the ends of the receiving blanket around each hand so I'd have a good grip, just waiting for a nod from Martin to choke this goofball.

Martin glanced back to see what I was doing, then looked forward hastily, his face convulsing with suppressed laughter.

"Say the word," I told him.

"Rory," Martin tried again. "Which one of you took Regina to the midwife's office?"

"Maybe I went part of the way," Rory improvised. "They dropped me off at the house on their way."

"And this baby, Hayden, the one in the backseat, is the child of Regina and Craig?"

"Gosh, I don't know. They all look alike, don't they?"

Martin turned a little and directed his next words at me. "You know, I'm actually tempted," he said. "Keep it handy."

Like most horrible things—roller coaster rides, committee meetings, vaginal exams—the trip eventually came to an end. After thirteen hours on the road (during two and a half of which Hayden screamed), we got to Corinth. By that time I didn't like anyone in the Mercedes, myself included. Rory directed Martin to his family's home, in a section of Corinth as derelict as any I'd seen in Lawrenceton. When we pulled up in front of a tiny brick house set up on a hill, the steps up to it steep and crooked, Rory ejected himself from the car with unflattering speed. "I'll give you a call," he promised. "Thanks for not turning me in. Take care of old Hayden, now." He went up the steps two at a time, his extra clothes clutched to him in a paper bag, his hair sticking out all around from a knit watch cap he'd had stuck in his pocket.

The streetlight gave the blond hair a tinge of green and his progress a definite touch of the surreptitious.

We watched him go with relief.

"If he had two thoughts at one time, they'd throw a surprise party," Martin said mysteriously, and I nodded.

"The question is, is he bad or good underneath the stupidity?" I said.

"I don't think he's smart enough to be bad," Martin said.

The same streetlight made my husband look hard and angry. Really, he was just tired and grumpy. Maybe.

"You don't have to be smart to be bad," I reminded him.

It was too late, and we were too tired, to cope with any surprises the farmhouse might have to offer. We checked into the Holiday Inn and staggered to our room with all the paraphernalia the baby required. Martin set up the portable crib while I changed Hayden, who rejected another bottle. There was a little refrigerator in the room, so I stuck the bottle in there, laid Hayden in the crib, and patted him on the back until he fell asleep. By that time, Martin was in bed. I felt like an elephant had rolled over on me and lain there for hours. I brushed my teeth, washed my face, and crawled in beside him.

Two hours later Hayden woke up.

I was standing beside the crib when I attained consciousness.

Hayden was hungry.

The formula was cold, and there was no way to heat it.

Finally, I tucked it in my nightgown next to my body—you can imagine how good that felt—and held Hayden and jiggled him in the room's straight chair, trying Binkys and bouncing and humming with no effect. When the formula was slightly less chilly, I stuck the nipple in Hayden's mouth, and after a brief protest, the baby began to suckle.

Martin slept all the way through this.

In the morning, when he shook me by the shoulder—very gently—I buried my face in the pillow.

"Roe," he said, kissing me on the cheek, "it's nine o'clock, and the baby's awake."

"Take care of him."

"I changed his diaper," Martin observed, trying not to sound proud and failing. "I think he's hungry, and there aren't any bottles."

"Go to the store, and see if they sell formula already made up," I advised. "Or take him to Craig's aunt and uncle and let them worry about it."

Martin heartlessly laid Hayden on the bed by me, and I raised my head enough to see his tiny finger waving. He made his little "eh" sound. His cheek was close enough to kiss, so I did, inhaling the now-familiar baby smell. I could hear the diaper rustle, and knew Martin hadn't put it on snugly enough. Oh, hell.

I sat up, groggy as it is possible to be. "I was up with him last night," I said, fixing Martin with as baleful a stare as I could scrape together. "While you slept," I emphasized, in case he hadn't gotten the point. I could not find any trace of sympathy for Martin in my heart. It didn't make any difference that his niece was missing and her husband dead. He'd had what I hadn't—undisturbed sleep.

"I'll go look," he said hastily. "What kind should I get?"

I made him write it down. Hayden was beginning to escalate in his demands. "And hurry," I added, in case he hadn't gotten *that* point.

There was no going back to sleep. I found a Binky, stuck it in Hayden's mouth, rejoiced to find that pacified him at least for the moment. I dashed into the bathroom, took a hot and sketchy shower, scrubbed my teeth again, and was appalled at the amount of makeup I needed to make myself look healthy this morning. I pulled on tobacco-brown slacks and a sweater of a deep yellow that I believed was called goldenrod. I took a moment to sit down on the bed and do some research with the local phone book. Then I finished rigging myself out with my rings, a chain, some earrings, my gold-rimmed glasses, and socks and loafers... By the time I'd finally put myself together, Martin was coming back in the room with a bag. It contained clean bottles and a few cans of ready-made formula.

"You wouldn't believe what I had to pay for this," he said with some indignation.

"I don't care. Did you get a can opener?" I asked tensely.

He produced one from the bag with an air of triumph, and I gave him a heartfelt kiss on the cheek. He was about to go for something more meaningful when I heard the warning tune-up behind me.

"He's getting serious," I said, panicking. "We've got to get the bottle ready now!"

Working together, we had a brand-new bottle full of brand-new formula ready in record time, and Hayden was gumming away on the nipple in blessed near-silence. While I aided and abetted, Martin checked the skinny Corinth telephone book for the address of Craig's family, the Harbors, who'd taken him in when his parents died.

"Maybe they're on their way to Lawrenceton," I said, with a wave of horror. "Maybe they're on their way there to collect Craig's body!"

"Nope," Martin said, his eyes never leaving the columns of phone numbers. "Padgett Lanier told me Craig's brother had asked him how to ship the body back to Corinth when the autopsy was over."

I felt a tide of relief sweep over me. The people who had raised Craig for the past five years were here in Corinth. I was not thinking of the Harbors as bereaved; I was thinking of them as baby repositories. And I'd lost any shame I had about it, too.

"Here they are," Martin said absently. "Eighteen-fifty-six Gettysburg Street." He closed the phone book and returned it to the drawer with a much more cheerful air.

"Who'd want to name a street after Gettysburg?" Obviously, I was talking right off the top of my head.

Martin looked up at me, his eyebrows raised and a patient look on his face.

"Oh," I said, abashed. I'm not one of those unreconstructed southerners who refers to the War of Northern Aggression, but it seemed I'd been indoctrinated to some extent. I made a face at my Yankee husband. These people probably had an Appomattox Avenue, too.

We packed all the baby's things in his diaper bag, folded up the crib for the last time, and went carefully down the stairs to our car. We hadn't had coffee yet, or breakfast, and yet that seemed secondary to getting Hayden to qualified caregivers.

Since Corinth is only a little bigger than Lawrenceton, we found the Harbors' house quickly. To my silent dismay, it seemed like a darker shadow of the place where we'd dropped off Rory the night before. This house's once-white siding was peeling, and the front yard had not a blade of grass.

Martin and I avoided looking at each other. We slowly got out of the car, and I opened the back door to extract Hayden. He was sound asleep, and I pulled out Ellen Lowry's blue-and-white-striped blanket to drape over his head. A chill rain had begun to fall. Martin covered us with an umbrella. We picked our way across the yard to the door. My heart sank at the sight of the ripped shades at the two front windows. Who could have guessed, seeing the Harbors at the wedding, that this was how they lived?

Then I chided myself for my snobbery, reminded myself that children grew up healthy and cherished in the poorest of homes. But I knew it wasn't the poverty that bothered me. It was the air that the people who lived under this roof had given up. They no longer cared—about peeling paint, or the lack of bushes to soften the mean lines of the old house, or the absence of stepping stones to keep visitors' feet dry on messy days. There was not even a two-dollar doormat outside the front door to wipe my feet on.

But someone had put a big black bow on the door knocker, to show that this was a house of mourning.

Martin leaned forward to rap on the wood and slid his arm around me. I leaned into its warmth, my hand absently patting Hayden's round little bottom.

I hardly recognized the woman who answered the door

as the same Lenore Harbor I'd met at the wedding. She'd put out a great effort then, I realized, seeing her now. Her hair had been done, her dress and shoes new. And she hadn't been smoking. A cigarette hung from the corner of her mouth now, jiggling when she spoke to us out of the other corner.

"I halfway expected you, Martin. Come on in, I guess. I haven't had a chance to clean up, I'm sure you know we've just been knocked on our butts by this news about Craig."

Her voice was raspy, but she didn't sound exactly as I'd expected. Sad, yes... but not agonized. She wasn't Craig's blood mother, of course. My heart began to sink.

I tried my hardest not to look around the room, but it was impossible not to absorb the depression that hung over the ancient furniture and loose linoleum, the plethora of overflowing ashtrays and discarded magazines. The Harbors had received a couple of plants and some sympathy cards, and they were arranged on the shelf of a nasty maple hutch. The ribbons on the arrangements stood out in brilliant contrast to the rest of the material in the dingy living room. But it wasn't the age of the furnishings, or even the presence of the ashtrays; it was the lack of maintenance, or care, of these things that bothered me.

This wasn't what I had pictured as a temporary home for Hayden.

"And this is your wife?"

Lenore Harbor had met me at the wedding, but didn't seem to recall that. Martin reintroduced me, and Lenore waved her hand at the couch. We perched there uneasily after piling all Hayden's gear near the door.

Lenore turned her head toward the back of the house and called, "Hugh! Martin and his little wife are here!"

There was a curious sound from the next room, a kind of long wheeze, and then Hugh Harbor made his way into the living room. He was preceded by the *thump! shuffle, thump! shuffle* of a person using a walker. Hugh was about Lenore's age, somewhere in his midfifties I estimated, and he was gaunt, with neutral coloring and light brown hair outlining a tonsure.

He greeted us in a wheezy voice. I noticed an oxygen tank sitting in the corner. Surely it was dangerous to smoke in a house with oxygen tanks? I remembered Rory saying that Hugh Harbor had been ill. I wished now I'd paid more attention, asked more questions. But in the rush to find someone to take Hayden off my hands, I hadn't thought enough ... about anything.

"I'm so glad you made the drive to come back to Corinth," Hugh Harbor said. I wondered how he knew we'd driven. He eased back into a green vinyl armchair with stuffing protruding from one arm. There was a towel spread over the seat. I suspected the towel covered worse depredations. "We don't think that Gina could've hurt poor Craig." Hugh wheezed. "Musta been some thief, don't you think? Or some guy who just saw Gina, thought she looked good? Craig wouldn't a let anyone mess with Gina."

"We're sure Regina didn't have anything to do with it," Martin agreed firmly. I could tell he was mighty relieved. It would have been horrible if they'd believed Regina had killed Craig.

"I know Hayden will be a consolation to you," I said,

but I couldn't hear any excitement in my voice. I sort of extended the baby, who'd been lying in my arms.

They gave me a very peculiar look, and I could tell they'd been married many years. Their faces held almost identical degrees of puzzlement and surprise.

"Of course, babies are wonderful things to have," Lenore said, with a distressing lack of enthusiasm. "Hugh and I raised a houseful of them. We didn't know you and Martin was even expecting, young lady."

Martin and I turned to look at each other. We probably had twin expressions too; and they were of sheer bafflement.

I didn't think I could talk, even if I could think of what to say. Martin looked down at Hayden, back at Lenore, who was taking advantage of the break in the conversation to light another cigarette.

"This isn't our baby," Martin said, not sounding very sure about it. "This is Craig and Regina's boy, Hayden."

You would have thought we'd announced we were going to strip and have sex on the floor. The Harbors once again had twin expressions—this time, shock and fascination. After they'd absorbed what Martin had said, emotions scudded across their faces like clouds on a windy day.

"This is the first we've heard of it," Lenore said finally. I could have sworn it wasn't the first thing she thought to say. Hugh nodded agreement, the top of his bald dome glinting in the overhead light as his head bobbed back and forth.

"You didn't know Craig and Regina were expecting a child?" Even knowing the answer, I had to ask. My heart couldn't have sunk further. It was at the level of my big toe.

"No," Hugh said. "They never said nothing about having a baby. Are you sure this boy is theirs?"

We did the Tweedledum and Tweedledee thing again, searching each other's faces. I gave a tiny shrug.

"That's what Regina told us," Martin said carefully. I had expected Martin to be visibly upset again, but to my relief, he had returned to his more familiar persona of cagey businessman. His face was unreadable; his hands loosely clasped each other in a relaxed way.

I gathered Hayden closer to my chest. I understood that I would be taking him out of this house with me. I looked at his little pile of paraphernalia and gave a silent sigh. All to be hauled back up the motel stairs again.

"How much did you see of Regina and Craig?" I asked, my voice as soft and simple as I could make it. Didn't want to put them on the defensive.

"Well, I ain't been well," Hugh said apologetically. "I have good spells. I was having one about the time they got married. But I ain't been so good since about late July, and I'm afraid I take up most of Lenore's time."

We had been fools to bring Hayden up here. I saw clearly that these people had not the resources, the legal obligation, or the slightest inclination to take care of Hayden even temporarily. How could we have been so blind? I had followed an anxious Martin's lead without a thought, consumed by my own conflicts. I should have listened to Angel; might have, if her baby hadn't decided that afternoon was the time to arrive. Angel had figured we should stay in Lawrenceton, and she'd been right.

I barely listened while the Harbors explained to Martin over and over again why they really hadn't had a chance to go visit the newlyweds since the wedding. The farm was far out in the country, they emphasized, and it was so hard for Hugh to get around. And, Lenore Harbor pointed out righteously, they hadn't been invited.

"Did Craig come to see you here?" Martin asked.

He'd dropped by once or twice, the Harbors admitted, usually with that friend of his, that Rory.

It took a few more questions from Martin to establish that the couple hadn't seen Regina—except across a store—since a week after the wedding. But they'd seen Craig quite often.

"You know," Hugh said with an effort, his breathing increasingly difficult, "we thought, when Craig got married—and we stood in as his folks at the wedding—we thought Craig's old ways were over. Gina being a little older than him, we thought she'd hold him down, make him toe the line. We were—well, I guess Lenore and I are maybe a little ashamed to say it—kind of relieved. Craig turned out to be a bigger responsibility than we ever dreamed, him getting into trouble so often. We was glad to take him in, Lenore being his aunt and so on, and we took care of him through high school, but I won't say it was all peaches and cream. We'd raised girls before, but that boy was a whole different kit and caboodle." He shook his shiny head sadly. "Nope, he and that Rory was always into trouble. We thought for a while that it was Rory who would marry Gina, when they began hanging around together."

Martin began our closing remarks, so to speak, and after a little more strained conversation, we rose to leave. We began tucking Hayden's bits and pieces wherever we could, with Martin once again holding the umbrella.

I nuzzled Hayden's fuzzy head, and wondered what we should do next.

As we pulled away from the broken curb, the silence in the Mercedes might well be described as thick. And tense.

I looked out at the passing streets of this depressing little farming town. I had no idea what Martin was thinking, but I knew if he asked me if I liked having a baby now that I had one, I would pinch him where it hurt, because I was so bitterly amazed at myself. I'd wanted a baby. Now I had one. And I was trying with all my might to get rid of him.

Partly, I thought, this was because the care of him had been dumped on me. Partly, it was because I hadn't had the hormonal buildup that natural mothers get.

But mostly, it was because I knew—I just knew—that his mother would turn up sooner or later, and Hayden would be gone. If the claimant wasn't Regina, it would be someone else with a better title to this child than mine, which was almost nonexistent. What point was there in lining up more pain for myself?

I felt better once I'd admitted all this in my secret heart. While we waited on a red light, I looked over at Martin, who was staring out the window at the bare trees. The sky had that leaden gray look that often presages snow, at least in my very limited experience.

"I guess we should talk to Cindy, and then Craig's brother," I said. I didn't sound excited about it.

"Yes, we need to," my husband agreed, turning to look across the seat at me. "And we need to track down Rory and see if we can get any more out of him. And we probably need to move our stuff out to the farmhouse. It'll be a lot easier with a stove and refrigerator. And more than one room." "It" being the care of Hayden, I gathered. I noticed we weren't saying one word about walking out of the Harbors' house with him, when we'd gone in with the resolve of leaving the baby with Craig's family.

"I wonder if the police have been out there, to the farm," I said, the idea sort of slipping into my head sideways.

Martin looked surprised, then thoughtful. "You'd think they'd want to see if anything Craig and Regina left out there could explain what happened," he said. "If the Lawrenceton sheriff's department called them. And I'm assuming they did." Martin mulled it over a little. "I know who to call. An old friend of mine named Karl Bagosian has a key to the house, and if anyone knows, he will."

We parked in front of the florist's shop owned by Cindy Bartell. I'd been there once before. Then, there had been Easter decorations in the big window facing the sidewalk. Now it was filled with fall decorations. Through that window, over the top of a miniature corn sheaf, I could see Cindy's head of smooth black hair bent over a gift basket on the large worktable behind the counter.

Martin was opening my car door, which he'd somewhat fallen out of the habit of doing. I had never seen door opening as an issue, but I used his choice as a clue to his feelings. As Martin held out his hand to help me out of the Mercedes, he looked down as if he were trying to refresh his memory of my face. I was all too aware that my hair had been excited by the rain into separating into streamers, with waves and curls interrupting their wild flow. My London Fog was not exactly a sexy garment, and I was sure my nose was shiny. I couldn't remember what glasses I'd put on this morning, so I reached up to touch the frames. The gold-tone wire rims.

"I was right," he said unexpectedly. Without further explanation, he unbuckled Hayden from the car seat in the back. He lifted the baby out, handed him to me, and in we went to interrupt his ex-wife's workday. The bell attached to the door ting-a-linged when we entered, and Cindy looked up.

"Martin, Aurora, how good to see you," Cindy said with a minimum of enthusiasm. "I see you survived the drive." She laid down the dried flowers she'd been working with, dusted her hands on her apron, and came around the counter. She actually shook hands with us, which I thought was a bit much. After all, she'd been married to Martin. She could've given him a little hug or something.

Then I noticed the large man just rising from a desk behind the counter. He got up, and up, stopping finally at about six-foot-five. He had a full mustache and dark hair peppered with gray, clipped even shorter than Cindy's. He also possessed a notable set of shoulders, and hands as big as my face. I found myself hoping he'd turn around so I could have a peek at the rear view.

"This is Dennis Stinson, Aurora," Cindy said, smiling. I'd never seen her smile. It made her look like a million dollars. I propped the baby over my shoulder so I could spare a hand for the hunk, and my fingers vanished in Dennis Stinson's. "Martin, I know you remember Dennis from high school."

"Of course. It's been a long time," Martin said, and I had to fight not to grin at the coolness in his voice.

"I guess this is the baby you were telling me about?" Cindy held out her arms, and I gently eased Hayden into them. She looked down at his flushed face, her discreetly made-up eyes scanning him.

"Cute kid," she said, and I exhaled silently. "You sure he's Regina's? I'd have put money on her telling me if she was expecting, Martin. It just seems incredible that someone as—well—dependent as Regina would do something as monumental as having a baby without telling the people who care about her."

I noticed Cindy didn't say it was unthinkable that Regina would stoop to such a deception.

"But we haven't seen her for the past few months, darling," Dennis rumbled. He had a voice that matched his size. "To tell you the truth, Martin, I didn't encourage Regina to come by here. She was always hitting Cindy up for money, or asking us to give Craig a job ... you get the picture. And since Cindy wasn't exactly a family member any more ..."

"Just the mother of Regina's cousin," Martin interjected quietly.

"Well, that, but not really Regina's aunt ..."

"How long had it been since you saw Craig or Regina?" I asked hastily, and Cindy looked a little surprised, as if she'd assumed I couldn't speak without permission.

"Oh ... what? Three months or so?" Cindy looked up at Dennis. "Regina came by the house," she continued.

"That was about the Fourth of July, so it was at least four months ago," Dennis said. "We were getting ready for our pool party."

"We were," Cindy confirmed with a reminiscent grin,

and I could feel my smile get broader. Cindy was apparently partnered with this hunk not only in a business sense, but also in a personal sense, and it certainly sounded like they were living together.

"She came by?" Martin prompted. "To the house on Archibald Street?"

"No, I moved. We moved. Dennis and I live on Grant."

I rolled my eyes. Gettysburg Street. Grant Street. "You *people,*" I muttered into the fuzz on Hayden's head.

"Did you say something, Aurora?" Dennis asked, bending down to me.

"No," I said, smiling with all the sugar in my system. "We're just having us a time, taking care of this little baby."

"Oh my gosh, Aurora, this must be awful for you!" I felt every muscle in my body tighten as her pitying tone alerted me to what she was about to say. "Is it true that you can't have your own? Martin, I think Barby told me you'd said that?" Cindy asked, and right then and there I decided I would kill my husband slowly, painfully, maybe publicly.

"Of course, with us never seeing Barrett, Martin was thinking of having more children," I said, as slowly and deliberately as I could manage. "But I said, 'No, Martin, that wouldn't hardly be fair to poor ol' Barrett. I know it doesn't look good, him never visiting you even though you've been sending him money for years, him never showing me the courtesy of shaking my hand—much less hugging my neck. But us having another child would just make Barrett feel so *bad.* So *displaced.*' " I stopped then, afraid I was over the line into parody.

Cindy turned an uneven kind of red.

Martin was looking at me with a kind of horrified fascination. I hoped he had enough sense to keep his mouth shut.

"So, where are you staying while you're in Corinth?" Dennis asked hastily.

"Ah—out at the old farm," Martin said, not taking his eyes off me. Evidently, he had enough sense. "We've been at the Holiday Inn, but with the baby... I think we would be better off out at the farm."

"It was nice of you to let Craig and Regina live there," Dennis said, since I was elaborately fussing with the baby and I had the strong feeling that Cindy was still staring at me.

"Yes," Martin said senselessly. "Well, we better be on our way. You wouldn't happen to know where Craig's brother Dylan lives, would you?"

Dennis said, "Let's step outside, Martin; I can give you better directions that way." They were out the door with suspicious alacrity. As Dennis pointed down the street, apparently counting stoplights, Cindy and I gave each other quick glances.

"Barrett really hasn't come to see you at all?" she asked in a subdued way.

"No. He doesn't acknowledge that I'm alive." To my pride, my voice was calm and dispassionate. "Now, I can see that is loyalty to you, which of course you'd expect from a son. But it does make Martin feel bad that Barrett never visits him and seldom calls."

His mother sighed heavily. "Barrett has never been able to see the divorce as anything but Martin walking out on us, though Barrett was in high school when we separated.

He never saw that if Martin needed to be away from me, I needed just as much to be away from him."

I tried to look interested and understanding. I was, to some extent, but I was also thinking my arms would fall off at the shoulders from the burden of holding this baby. I sort of half laid Hayden on the glass-topped counter.

"Just before and after her marriage, Regina used to come talk to me," Cindy went on in a low voice, while through the front window I observed Dennis and Martin continue their pantomime of checking the weather and kicking the tires, or whatever guys do when women have embarrassed them. "Aurora, there's something wrong with that girl. She's got some moral blind spots. Craig's brushes with the law seemed to make no difference to her whatsoever, and the fact that Rory went everywhere with Craig—and I mean *everywhere*—didn't seem to give her any pause."

Hayden's Binky rolled from his mouth. Even as he made some fussy protest, Cindy caught it in her hand before it hit the floor and popped it back into the little mouth. Hayden lapsed back into semiconsciousness.

"What do you mean?" I asked cautiously. "Good catch, by the way."

"Thanks. I guess I mean Regina never seemed to make a moral judgment about the trouble Craig got into, he and Rory. She never said, 'Oh, no, my husband has done a bad thing, writing those worthless checks.' Or 'My God, my husband uses illegal drugs!' And she never tried to defend him either . . . pretend he was set up, or he was simply innocent. It was like it was just a lark, you know? Just fun. And ah-oh, Craig got caught!"

I'd always just thought Regina was intellectually stupid. According to Cindy, she was morally stupid as well.

"Thanks for warning me, Cindy," I said. I took a deep breath and tried a social smile. "Dennis seems very nice."

"Oh..." she paused, eyed me sideways in a significant way. "He *is*."

We both started laughing, and Cindy opened the door for me. At the sound of the bell, the men both turned with relief apparent on their faces. Martin unlocked the Mercedes.

"You might want to call Margaret and Luke Granberry when you get out to the farm," Dennis suggested. "They've owned the one next door for a few months. Luke pretends to farm, and Margaret pretends to farm right along with him. They're really living on income from a trust, but they're trying to put a back-to-nature spin on it."

"They're very nice," Cindy agreed. "She's the kind of woman who loves to help out."

Martin and I nodded our thanks for the information, went through the interminable process of buckling Hayden in his seat, and finally were back on the street.

I took a deep breath. "Martin," I began.

"Roe," he forestalled me. "Listen, I know, I'm sorry. I had no right to tell Barby your problems. I was just—unhappy that you were unhappy, and she asked me over the phone one night how you were. I just... overstepped my bounds."

"Yes."

"You and Cindy were having your difficulties, weren't you?"

"We're okay now, Martin. I don't want to go relate our whole conversation."

"You and Cindy are at peace?"

"Yes."

"What about you and me?"

"Unless you ask me first, never tell anyone about my female problems. Never."

"I promise."

"Okay. We're all right."

"You don't sound altogether all right."

"Don't push it."

We stopped at Dylan Graham's house next. After the squalor of the Harbors' place, Craig's brother's home was almost painfully respectable. It was small, and on a street of small houses. But every yard was neat, and Dylan's house in particular was freshly painted and shiny. The only disorder, if you could call it that, was the scattering of toys visible in the little backyard. I remembered Rory telling us that Dylan and his wife had a little girl.

Rory, come to think of it, had been full of information, of the less-than-valuable-and-pertinent kind.

Martin went to the front door and knocked. After a long pause, the door opened, and a young woman began talking to Martin. At first her face looked suspicious and tight, but gradually she seemed to relax. She was plump and plain and friendly, with a small mouth, pale freckled skin, and crinkled light brown hair that was cut in bangs in the front and bushed out behind her shoulders.

Martin turned and gestured to me to come on, and I slipped out of the car and started to walk toward the little house.

And then I remembered the baby. I heaved a sigh, the theatrical kind, and turned around to go through the process of retrieving Hayden.

"Oh, isn't he beautiful!" the young woman said. "Won't you come in?"

While we exchanged condolences on the death of her brother-in-law, she waved us into the tiny house, which reminded me of an apartment I'd had while I was in college. The complex had just been finished when I signed the lease, and everything in the small space had gleamed: kitchen cabinets, walls, countertops. Craig's older brother, Dylan, and his wife, Shondra, were obviously house-proud, and after a few days of taking care of an infant, I was impressed that Shondra, herself a new mother, was still keeping her standards high.

Shondra was just as spotless as her house; her face was scrubbed, making me feel like a made-up tramp, her rose-tinted sweats were pristine, and even her sneakers were spanky white.

"Such a nice home," I said quietly, after she'd talked about Craig a little, without much sorrow. Shondra beamed, her conventional expression of grief shucked in a second.

"Thank you," she said, trying to sound offhand. "Dylan did most of the work on it himself, in the evenings and on weekends."

"That must have been hard," Martin commented. He had taken off his coat and was holding the baby while I tugged mine at the sleeves.

"Well, I didn't get to see a lot of him. So I'd come over with his supper or a snack and just sit and watch, while I was expecting," Shondra said, a little smile letting us know she'd enjoyed that.

"Where's your little girl?" I asked politely.

"Kelly. She's taking a nap," Shondra said. "Can I hold this little guy? My brother was just here, and I wanted to thank you for bringing him home."

Martin and I glanced at each other. We were sure slow on the uptake.

Martin, who'd had more sleep, heard the shoe drop first. "Rory? Rory Brown is your brother?"

Shondra looked down at the baby, rocking him gently in her round arms. "Yes," she admitted, less happily. "Rory is my big brother. He's, ah, he's . . . a good-natured guy, and Dylan and I have been praying hard that he'll see the Lord's ways."

I looked at the little table sitting in the exact middle of the kitchen. There were two mugs on it, one with a spoon beside it with a little circle of brown in the center. The coffee wasn't dry yet.

"We must have just missed him?" I held out my hands, offering to take Hayden back. Shondra noted my gesture but she stared down at his face for several more long seconds, as if she'd just noticed something that gave her pause.

"Oh, that's right. You just missed him," she said absently. "In fact, when we heard your car pull up, he went right out the back door." Shondra glanced over at some pictures and a vase of dried flowers on top of the composite oak-colored TV cabinet, then back to the baby's face. She slowly returned Hayden to me. "He's a beautiful baby," she said soberly. Her small mouth pursed, as if she was thinking over a problem.

A little wail from the back of the house pulled at her attention like a tractor beam. "My goodness, Kelly is up. Let me go see to her."

While Shondra was out of the room, I strolled over to the TV cabinet as casually as I could manage. The framed baby pictures were old enough to be from Shondra's family album, or Dylan's, and in one grouping was a baby girl about a year old, a baby girl embedded in a ruffled dress with a little bow stuck in her wispy hair, and a baby boy in a tiny suit. "Barf," I muttered, and then the face of the baby caught my eye.

"Hmmm and double hmmm," I muttered, turning away right before Shondra came back in carrying a much larger bundle than Hayden.

While we were doing the obligatory admiring of the child, I was nasty enough to be sorry this young couple already had a baby, so perfect would they be to leave Hayden with. And they were blood relations to the baby, one way or the other. Martin and I had not discussed the possibility of finding a temporary home for Hayden with Dylan and Shondra, and after the shock of the Harbors' house, I would've been scared to even mention it before I'd met them.

As it was, I hadn't met Dylan. After a few minutes' conversation with Shondra, I could see the steel beneath the sweetness and lack of worldliness that were undoubtedly genuine. So it was my impression that Shondra would not marry a charming ne'er-do-well like her brother, or a true rascal like her brother-in-law. But we'd have to check Dylan out, and we could hardly be sure that they'd agree to something as difficult as taking care of another baby.

Martin and I exchanged glances. He'd read my mind. He asked a few questions about Dylan's job at the John Deere dealership, which I knew would give him an idea about Dylan's income and hours, and he got more information out of Shondra about her brother than I would have thought possible.

"Shondra, excuse me, I was just wondering," I interjected, when Martin showed signs of flagging and Shondra was asking us for the third time if she could get us a drink. "Did you know your sister-in-law was pregnant?"

Shondra's face flooded with guilty color. "Yes, ma'am," she blurted, as though she'd been caught in a shameful position. "She called me on the phone and told me, about a month before the baby was due."

"Did you see her while she was pregnant?"

"No, ma'am."

I felt as old as the hills because of that "ma'am," and I had to nip at the inside of my mouth to keep from protesting.

"Did you know when she had the baby?"

"My brother said she had," Shondra said, fussing unnecessarily with the baby's plastic keys. Her baby grabbed the ring and stuffed it into her mouth, gumming the toy enthusiastically. "Oh, honey, that ain't real clean," Shondra muttered to the baby, but let the child keep it.

I noted that Shondra had not said that she'd seen Regina when Regina was obviously pregnant. So far, no one reliable had admitted to that. "Do you know where Regina had this baby?" I asked.

"You sure you couldn't drink some hot chocolate?"

"No, thank you," Martin said, quite firmly. He was getting impatient, because he was accustomed to people telling him what he needed to know, telling him promptly and in detail. I sent him one of those looks that say *back off.*

"Did she have Hayden at the local hospital?" I asked, to get us back on the track.

"No, ma'am. Rory said she went to the midwife in Brook County."

That was what he'd told us.

"And her name is?" I smiled at Shondra as coaxingly as I can smile.

"Her name is Bobbye Sunday," Shondra said, looking down at the baby fixedly. She spoke so unwillingly that I knew she was telling us the truth.

"Thank you," Martin said, letting out a pent-up breath and practically jumping up from his chair. He swept the diaper bag up with one hand and held out his other hand to me. I accepted a little yank, to get me up off the couch with Hayden. We said our good-byes and thanks in a flurry of goodwill and relief that this visit was over, and at Martin's request Shondra promised to send Dylan out to see us that afternoon when he got off work. Martin strongly suggested that Dylan bring Rory with him.

We returned to the Holiday Inn, gathered our belongings, and checked out, each separately reviewing our little visit mentally. Rory was avoiding us, which meant he had information he didn't want to give us. That wasn't exactly news, but it was interesting. Martin hadn't agreed to bring the young man back to Corinth, in direct violation of the law and common sense, just to have him skip out on us and avoid us at every turn, and I had to promise myself a new pair of glasses if I didn't let the phrase "I told you so" cross my lips.

I ran into the grocery briefly, and while I shopped, Martin bravely took Hayden with him into K-Mart. Then we were on our way to the farm where Martin had grown up, where he'd lived until he'd gone to Vietnam. His father had died when Martin was a boy, and by the time Martin left Corinth, his mother had been married for years to another farmer, Joseph Flocken. It was the widowed Joseph I'd had to see in order to purchase the farm I'd given back to Martin as a wedding present.

The Bartell farm was south of town on Route 8, further out than I remembered. You could just see a bit of the roof from the road. "Secluded" was the word for this property, if you were feeling charitable. Actually, the farm seemed forlorn and bleak, out here in the winter countryside. As we reached the end of the long gravel driveway, I saw that Martin had indeed had the house restored. It was trim and painted now, and the barn had been leveled, so there was no longer a blight on the landscape. The driveway had been regraveled, too, and we pulled up to the side of the house under a new carport. It was just a roof on four posts, but it would keep the worst of the snow and rain off the car.

As best I remembered, there were three ground-floor doors: the front door, covered by a tiny roof, the kitchen door to the side, and the back door, which led onto a small porch-cum-laundry room that was now glassed in. Martin had the door keys on his key ring—another surprise. I found it interesting and strange that the keys to the old farmhouse were always by his hand.

"Is there a phone?" I asked.

"I don't know. I should've called Karl before we left

town. He'd know. I've always got the cell phone if we have to use it."

I waited at the bottom of the kitchen steps, Hayden a bundle of blankets in my arms, while Martin fumbled with the key. Finally the door yielded, and we stepped into the house.

"How long has it been since you were here?" I asked cautiously, looking around at the room. The kitchen had been scrubbed and repainted, and the counters had new surfaces since I'd toured it so briefly years before. The overhead light was on, and there was a plate on the table. It still held food. It had been there for days. The glass beside it was half full of Coke, or one of the other dark cola drinks.

"Not since it was finished. I came to look at it once, when I had to be in Pittsburgh for business. And I got the cleaners and contractors out here to tell them what to do, though it was Karl who checked on their work for me. I haven't been in here since then, and I think that was at least a year and a half ago. I told Regina when she married Craig that the house was sitting empty and since they were going to be in Corinth for a while, they might as well use it. Barby had been hinting how hard up they were going to be."

I wandered slowly through the downstairs, deciding the house was even older than ours in Georgia. The old window coverings—I remembered them as ragged blinds—had been thrown away, and Regina hadn't replaced them. The gray sky outside seemed to fill the rooms with gloom. While Martin brought in the rest of our things, I walked around with Hayden.

I had very little memory of the house, but today I

discovered that in that memory I had minimized the size of the rooms and maximized the height of the ceiling. Martin's childhood home was an old two-story farmhouse, with three large rooms downstairs and three up; a decent bathroom on each floor that had obviously been created from a small bedroom or large closet; a large original pantry off the kitchen; and a washer and dryer crammed on the added glassed-in back porch. I was betting that had first been called a mudroom.

If Joseph Flocken had left anything in the house, Martin had had it cleaned out.

The plaid couch and matching armchair in the family room were surely out of someone's attic, probably Barby's, and the lone bed upstairs with its matching night tables and chest of drawers had been Barby's wedding gift to the couple, I recalled. I opened the closet door. Clothes, not many. Mostly flannel shirts and blue jeans, for both Craig and Regina.

I wondered where Regina was now. It made me shiver, seeing those clothes hanging there.

But I shoved them over to one side of the closet, making room for our hanging bag. Awkwardly, one-handed due to Hayden, I stripped the sheets off the bed. I tossed them down the stairs so I could pick them up and wash them later.

I heard Martin rumbling around on the ground floor, doing God knows what. I thought of calling to him, but instead I wandered into the second bedroom upstairs, across the little landing.

There was a sleeping bag on the floor, with a pile of clothes beside it. More blue jeans and flannel shirts, and

T-shirts, socks, underwear. A pair of heavy boots. There was a door between this bedroom and the next.

"Hmmm," I said. "Whose are those, Hayden?" Hayden made one of his favorite "eh!" sounds in response, and waved his hands. Martin was standing beside me suddenly, but I was used to his quiet approaches and wasn't too startled. He had a box under his arm.

"Rory stayed here, I'll bet," he said, and we exchanged looks. Hugh Harbor's remark about not knowing whether Regina would marry Craig or Rory had stuck with both of us. And while she and I were alone, Cindy had hinted pretty heavily that Craig and Rory did everything together. I saw no need to pass that little tidbit along to my husband.

"It probably wouldn't have done any good, but we should have asked him more questions when we had him," I commented, and then bit my lip. I was getting mighty close to losing my new glasses.

"Yes," said Martin heavily. "We should. I'm going to try to track him down tomorrow, if Dylan doesn't bring him out this afternoon."

When we moved on to the next room, which also opened onto the common landing as well as connecting with this bedroom, we found it contained a battered, aged crib (cadged from the Salvation Army or some garage sale, I was willing to bet) and an equally dilapidated rocking chair. There were none of the accouterments I'd seen in my friends' nurseries: no mobile, no changing table, no diaper pail. There was an old plastic garbage can, cracked and dirty, still with rolled-up dirty diapers inside. The sheet in the crib appeared to be a regular twin flat, sloppily folded and tucked to fit the small mattress.

"She didn't really plan on keeping a baby here." I turned to face Martin. With reluctance, he met my eyes.

"There aren't any presents," I said mercilessly. "You always get presents when you have a baby. Even kids living on the poverty edge get presents when they have a baby—maybe just a crib sheet or a receiving blanket from the dollar store, but they get something pretty. This, this is *nothing.* There's no way on earth she planned on keeping this baby. I'll bet she wasn't ever really pregnant."

"What about the things she brought to our house?"

"The diaper bag and the portable crib?" I took a deep breath. "The tags were still on. I think on her way to our house, she stopped at the first discount store she came to and charged them or wrote a bad check for them," I said. "Or maybe she took those things from whoever she took this baby from."

Martin flinched.

"We have to talk about it, Martin. No one knew she was pregnant. She didn't go the hospital. Rory just says Craig took her to a midwife. Did you notice how reluctant Shondra was to tell us what the midwife's name was? I'll bet if we ask this Bobbye Sunday, she'll tell us that Regina was never a patient. How do we know this baby is even Regina's? What if—well, what if the money in the diaper bag was ransom money?"

"Rory knew the birth weight," Martin said. "You remember, in the restaurant, when the waitress asked?"

I nodded. "I also know Rory's a liar." Hayden raised his head off my shoulder and goggled at the room. I turned my head slightly and kissed his cheek. His face wobbled around to mine. He banged his skull against my shoulder, and then came up again to look at me. We rubbed noses. His eyelids fluttered, and he laid his head down on my shoulder again.

"I don't know who bore this baby," Martin said, his fingers brushing Hayden's wisp of hair. "But I think Rory was around when it happened."

"So, we need to talk to the midwife. And we need to find out if Craig's big brother knew more about it than his wife did." I was swaying gently from side to side, assisting Hayden's slide into sleep. I eased over to the crib, glared down at the sheet, certain it was dirty. In a whisper, I asked Martin to lay one of our receiving blankets over it. When he'd done that, I eased the baby into the crib, propping him on his side with a small firm pillow at his back, and covering him with one of the blankets Ellen had given me.

I'd been aware Martin was still in the room, and I stepped quietly over to see what he was doing squatting on the floor.

Martin was plugging in a brand-new nursery monitor he'd extracted from the box he'd had under his arm. He untwisted the tie around the cord and moved the transmitter close to the crib. Wordlessly, he handed me the receiver. He'd already put batteries inside. I looked up at him, and his face told me clearly I better not comment on his acquisition. He must have bought it on his trip to K-Mart this morning.

Martin and I left the room on tiptoe, and half closed the door behind us. The house had been cold when we entered. Since Craig and Regina had been paying their own gas bill, they'd kept the heat turned down, or maybe his friend Karl had lowered the thermostat, but Martin had gone straight to it and moved it up. He stood in the nearly bare living room, looking around him at the gleaming wood of the floors and the soft white of the walls. I knew the memories must be flooding in. As I watched him, I saw him change, the years erase. There were traces in his face of things I never saw on the man I'd married: uncertainty, unhappiness, doubt.

In three quick steps I'd reached him and put my arms around him. I wished I were taller so he could rest his head against my chest and feel protected, just for a moment. It was an awful thing, being a man, I thought; and I pitied Martin for the first time since I'd known him.

With Hayden asleep, we were able to explore the house a little more thoroughly. I opened cabinets and drawers, feeling like the worst kind of snoop, since Regina had arranged all these things in her own system. But I couldn't see a way around it. We'd be here for at least a few days, and we might as well use what was there; it was Martin's house, after all, and Regina's child was with us. Well, a child, maybe Regina's.

Craig and Regina's belongings fell into two categories, like most young married couples'. They had old things given them by relatives and friends who no longer wanted them, like the couch and chair in the living room and some rather battered pots and pans; and they had brand-spanking-new things they'd gotten for wedding presents. Regina's engraved thank-you notes were still sitting underneath an address book in the kitchen drawer that held the phone book and quick-phone list.

While Martin wandered around checking out the renovation job, and probably reminiscing, I located kitchen things I might need, figured out the stove, and started lunch. Corinth didn't have much in the way of restaurants, and I didn't feel like coping with Hayden in a public place again. Besides, I like to cook, especially when no one else is in the kitchen. I planned a large meal since we'd missed breakfast. When Martin saw me deboning chicken breasts, he pulled on his coat and scarf and went outside to take a walk. He returned with the welcome news that in case we needed it, there was a rack of firewood that looked dry.

I thought about Darius Quattermain when Martin mentioned the firewood. I wondered if he was all right, if he would ever feel like delivering wood to my house again. Maybe no one had told him he'd stripped in front of me, but he might remember all on his own. I didn't know what drug he'd taken, or what its after-effects would be. As I waited for the cooking oil to heat in the electric skillet, I wondered what kind of person would drug another; it was a kind of poisoning, wasn't it? Poisoners were supposed to be sly and patient, I recalled. Anyone could pick up a baseball bat and swing it out of frustration. Well, maybe not anyone, but many people. I was sure the number of potential poisoners in the population must be much lower.

"What are you thinking of?" Martin asked, and I jumped, dropping the chicken breast into the hot oil, which popped me. When he'd apologized and I'd taken my hand out from under the cold running water, I said, "I was just thinking about Darius."

"You were shaking your head, raising your eyebrows in this kind of amazed look, and got this *ew* expression on your face."

I shook my head, feeling silly. I didn't want to explain my train of thought to Martin. A knock at the front door made me jump again. Martin went to answer it, and a second later a tall young man came with him into the kitchen. I had only to look at his face for a moment to know this was Craig's brother.

I wiped my hands on a dish towel and took Dylan's hand, telling him how sorry I was.

Dylan, who was wearing a John Deere green shirt and some khakis, was dark like his brother, but his build wasn't reedy like Craig's had been. Dylan was more bull-like, solid and stolid, a man who saw his way from Point A to Point B and took the most direct route.

"I would sure like to see the baby," he told me, and seemed surprised when Martin volunteered to take him upstairs to the makeshift nursery.

When they came back, Dylan looked like a man with a puzzle in front of him.

He accepted a seat at the old kitchen table, folded his hands on it, and began to say what he'd come to say.

"I couldn't set my hands on Rory to bring him with me. Shondra told me you wanted to talk to him."

Since he said this primarily to Martin, Martin nodded. I kept on pottering around the kitchen, feeling this would make the younger man relax a little more. I opened a can of green beans, put them in a very nice saucepan, and began to cook the rice in the microwave (chipped Corningware casserole, aged small microwave).

"My brother, Craig," Dylan began, and came to a difficult silence. We both kept our eyes down, waiting patiently. "My brother, Craig, was not always a good man."

Martin made a gesture that could be interpreted as "Who is?" and I made a little noise that was meant to be commiserating. This seemed to encourage Dylan.

"Craig likes—liked—things to be easy. But being married and earning a living—being an adult—those aren't easy things."

I nodded to myself. That was the absolute truth.

"I'm the last person Craig would have told, if he'd had plans to somehow make money off that poor little baby. But I can't help fearing somehow that was the case. Whatever Craig's plans were, Rory knows them. I hate to speak bad about my wife's brother, just like she didn't like to speak bad about Craig, but the fact is, Rory and Craig are two of a kind, and they deserved each other, just the way I hope Shondra and I deserve each other. If you had Rory in the car with you all the way here, I guess that was your best chance to find out what he knew. I don't pretend to understand why you let him go. Why didn't you turn him over to the police?"

Oooh, good question. I raised my eyebrows inquiringly and transferred my attention to Martin.

"At the time," Martin answered, thinking as he spoke, "I was sure that bringing him here would make things go easier on Regina if the police picked her up. I think—I know—I was sure Regina had killed Craig, and I didn't want to see her in jail, see her stand trial. Particularly since I couldn't understand why. Why she would do that, how she would do that. Regina is the most important thing in my sister's life, she's ..." My husband seemed to run out of words.

"But letting her get away with murder ain't doing her a favor," Dylan said.

Martin and I blinked and looked at him.

There was not a thing to say.

He was absolutely right.

7

We had more company that evening. After a quiet afternoon, we'd had a light supper. I'd just washed the supper dishes. Martin, in between trying to get in touch with the midwife and with Rory Brown (we'd found a working phone), had boiled a used batch of bottles and nipples and set them out to drain on a clean towel. I'd put a load of linens and a few clothes through the washing-and-drying cycle. The isolated position of the farmhouse had begun to make me think of us as cut off from the world, a not-unpleasant idea; so the sound of the car and the knock at the front door came as something of a jolt.

Martin walked through the living room to the front door and switched on the outside light. There wasn't a peephole, and the door was solid wood with no glass window, so he just had to open the door on trust, a habit we'd discarded. Big-city crime was drifting from Atlanta through outlying suburbs like Lawrenceton at an alarming rate.

I don't think Martin could have looked very welcoming, but the couple on the steps didn't seem alarmed. They were smiling in a friendly way, and they maintained their smiles even when faced with Martin's stern expression.

I ventured out into the living room when I heard the man say, "Hi! I'm Luke Granberry, and this is my wife, Margaret. We have the farm to the south of here."

"Martin Bartell." My husband held out his hand and Luke shook it exactly the right amount.

"We can just barely see the farm from our house, and we noticed more lights on tonight than there have been, so we felt we ought to check it out," Margaret said. Luke Granberry seemed to be about thirty or so, and Margaret was within five years of that, more or less, I estimated. The closer I got to her, the stronger I was willing to bet on the "more."

Hers was the most beautiful skin I'd ever seen, pale and smooth as silk, with fine webbing at the corners of her eyes and mouth. Her hair was red, flaming red, bushy and full. She wore it pulled back from her forehead with a cheap barrette. As she bent to shake my hand, I noticed she wore no jewelry besides her plain wedding ring.

"Please come in," I said. "I'm Martin's wife, Aurora."

Martin stood aside to let the neighbors in. As Luke Granberry edged past Martin, I could see that our visitor was the taller and broader. He had huge shoulders and a mildly handsome face, distinguished mostly by high cheekbones that made his small brown eyes seem perpetually scanning the distance for some adventure. His dark hair and brown eyes made his wife look even paler.

"Regina told us about you," Margaret said. "The aunt and uncle, right?"

"Yes, I'm Regina's mother's brother," Martin said.

"Barby's brother," Luke said. He looked at Martin as if trying to see a trace of Regina in his face. "We heard a rumor that there was some problem . . . ?" Luke spread his big hands in a gesture that seemed to imply that the Granberrys wanted to help, if only they knew how.

"Regina is missing," I said. Unfortunately, because I didn't know these people and so couldn't burden them with our emotions, I sounded like Regina's disappearance was just a little whim of hers. I was sorry the minute the words left my mouth.

"We're sure she'll turn up just any time," Martin said, to give me some support. *We really do care, we just have a positive attitude,* his voice implied.

"Where are Craig and Rory?" Margaret asked, looking around the room as if she expected we'd stuck them in a corner.

"Please come in and have a seat," I said, glancing anxiously at Martin. "I'm afraid we have some bad news about Craig." I had no idea if these neighbors had known Craig well, and could not gauge how much preparation they needed for the bad news.

Since there was only the couch and one chair in the living room, seating was a pretty cut-and-dried process. The Granberrys took the couch, which I indicated with a hostessy sweep of my hand, and I perched on the edge of the chair so my feet could touch the floor, Martin standing just behind me. I looked back at Martin, but his face gave away nothing.

"Ah... Craig is dead, I'm afraid." I gave them my most serious expression, which Martin always said looked as though I suspected I was having a heart attack.

"Oh, it's true, he's dead!" Margaret said. She turned to her husband, the thick red hair sweeping across her shoulders. Her white hands clutched his. "Luke!"

"I'm so sorry," Luke Granberry said, in a slow and solemn voice that I thought would be perfect for reading Poe out loud. I hastily put a cap on that thought, since I'd actually opened my mouth to say it, and instead pursed my lips and shook my head, as if the tragedy were too horrible for words.

"So you'd already heard?" Martin asked.

"The counterman at the hardware store said he'd heard it from Hugh Harbor, yes. But we didn't think we knew the Harbors well enough to call and ask them what the facts were. We heard Hugh is really sick ... and we didn't see Craig's funeral announcement in the paper."

"The body hasn't been released by the medical examiner yet," I said, finally managing to strike the right tone. Sober concern, that was appropriate. For the first time, I realized I was sleep deprived in a serious way. As if hearing his psychic cue, Hayden began to make noises upstairs. It was amazing how clearly his little voice came over the receiver, which I was clutching in my left hand. I'd been afraid to put it down.

I half turned to Martin, said, "I'll check, honey," (as though Martin had moved). I plodded up the stairs, to see the little arms and legs flailing above the edge of the bumper pads.

He wasn't crying, so I figured he wasn't hungry. Maybe you were supposed to hold off on the bottle until they asked for it? Since the only way for a baby to ask for a bottle was to cry, wasn't that kind of mean? On the other hand, sticking food in their mouth every time they were awake would create a bad pattern ... Gosh, there was nothing easy about this. You might as well get your answers by interpreting the pattern of chicken bones tossed under the full moon. I propped Hayden back on his side and began to pat him. To my pleasure, he went back to sleep.

While I'd been tending to Hayden, the Granberrys had been establishing common ground with Martin. I'd hoped they'd be a source of information about Regina and Craig, but I knew we'd have to let a polite conversational time lapse before questioning them. They'd been talking about the possibility of snow during the night, and I came in on the tail end of the weather discussion.

Margaret liked babies. I could tell by the way her eyes latched onto the nursery monitor as I came into the room.

"I didn't realize you and Martin were parents," she said slowly. "How old is your baby?"

Martin, who'd gotten a straight chair from the kitchen, looked resigned.

I said, "He isn't ours." After they refused a drink, I eased back into the chair, tired as I'd ever been in my life.

"You're baby-sitting?"

"This is Regina's baby," Martin said.

"*Regina's* baby?" If such a thing were possible, the pale Margaret, whom I was beginning to warm to, turned a shade whiter. She stared at us, stunned.

Even her next-door neighbors hadn't known Regina was going to have a baby? My doubt that Regina had ever given birth was beginning to consume me.

"Regina's baby?" Luke asked. He seemed just as startled as his wife. "Where on earth has it been?"

"With Regina missing and Craig dead, we had to step in," Martin said smoothly, as I opened my mouth to tell them the whole story.

"That was the best plan," I said, just to justify my open mouth.

Obviously, the Granberrys were curious, but too polite to ask any more questions. After some idle talk about how long we might stay, and a polite offer on our visitors' part to help in any way they could, the Granberrys rose to leave. Margaret was holding Luke's hand, and I thought that was sweet. I love to see people who've been married a while still act like lovers.

Though, I considered, she might actually need the support. Margaret was looking a little shaky.

"We didn't know Regina was going to have a baby," I said, kind of throwing out a line, as Luke and Martin were shaking hands.

Margaret nodded. "She was very secretive about it, apparently. Listen, if you get lonely, give me a call? Our number's in the book. If Martin has catching up to do with friends here in town, you may be at loose ends. Or maybe you'll need me to baby-sit."

"Thank you," I said. "I'll call you. And thanks for coming to check on the house. We appreciate your being concerned."

"We've tried to keep an eye on the house since we heard about Craig," Luke said. He looked from Martin to me, to make sure we both understood his sincerity. "If you need anything, anything, while you're here, just let us know. We'll be glad to see you."

As I gave Hayden his bottle later, I said, "They seemed nice, Martin. I think we should try to get together with them again and see if they know any more about Craig and Regina than the little we know. It sounded to me like they saw them fairly often. What do you think?"

"They seem too damn trusting," my husband said. "Coming all the way over to what they think may be an empty house at night, to check on lights. What if we'd been burglars?"

"He had a rifle in the gun rack in the cab of his pickup," I said, moving Hayden to my shoulder to burp him. "I noticed, because it made me feel right at home." In Lawrenceton, everyone seemed to own a gun, a rifle, or a shotgun, whether or not they hunted. Martin had a gun himself; Martin had not always been a business executive, as I would do well to remind myself.

This day had contained more than its fair share of hours. I was ready for it to be over. The ancient dryer was taking too long to dry the newly washed sheets. Martin occupied Hayden while I went in search of more. I was surprised and relieved to find another set in the upstairs bathroom closet, and it took me a minute or two to remake the bed. I had to put on the same blankets and bedspread, but I resolved to wash them in the morning.

I knew, as I scrubbed quickly in the ancient bathtub, that any mild obligatory affection I had had for Regina had ebbed away with this close examination of her marriage. I loathed her life. I loathed her little mysteries. But most of all, I loathed the nasty situation she'd dragged to our door, because I had a deep conviction that Regina had known exactly how imperiled she was when she'd driven from Corinth to Lawrenceton. If she'd been open with us, if she'd been frank, everything that had happened since then—and I visualized a long set of dominos, one toppling against the other—could have been prevented.

My distaste and disapproval for a member of Martin's

family made me feel like a bad Christian and a bad wife. I'd often thought being a Christian meant by definition being a bad one, since nothing is more difficult than Christianity, so I was more or less used to that feeling. But I was not used to being a bad wife.

Maybe I could make it up to Martin, a little.

He was dozing when I crawled in bed next to him. I'd switched off the light in the bathroom off the landing, and making my way to the bed was something of an adventure. But once there, he wasn't hard to find. I slid down, down under the covers. Martin made a startled noise. But it was definitely on the happy-startled side.

Afterward, when he held me and kissed me, he murmured, "Oh, honey, that was so good."

"I hope I haven't made you crazy today," I ventured.

"You've made me crazy from the moment I laid eyes on you," he told me, his voice drowsy with sleep and satisfaction.

I snuggled into my pillow, praying for a Hayden-less night.

"I love you," Martin said suddenly. "I have a feeling that's gotten shunted to a sidetrack the past few days."

Past few months, more like.

"I know you love me," I whispered.

"When we got married..."

I was so exhausted I had to force myself to listen. None of the Advice to the Lovelorn columns told you that some days you'd be too sleepy to listen to a declaration of love.

"...all I wanted was to protect you from any harm. To make you safe. Not to let anything worry you... frighten you... and make sure you never wanted for anything."

Bless his heart, that was just not possible. But it was the most attractive illusion in the world, wasn't it? What had I wanted to give Martin in return? I remembered hazily that I'd resolved to help him in his career by being a good hostess and a good guest, attending every event promptly and in appropriate clothes, expressing appropriate sentiments. I'd wanted to provide him with a house that was a home: clean, comfortable, good cooking smells in the kitchen, laundered clothes.

But after a while I'd felt compelled to work at least part-time, to go back to the library, because I loved the job and the books and the people. And there were days I had indulged myself by reading rather than doing the laundry, talking to my mother and my friends rather than starting preparations for an elaborate meal. And since I had a big contrary streak running all the way through me, I had sometimes rebelled in my own tiny way by wearing bizarre glasses to a Pan-Am Agra wives dinner, or by saying what I actually thought rather than what people wanted to hear.

"So," I said suddenly, "have I been the wife you wanted?"

"I didn't want 'a wife,' " he muttered, clearly putting the phrase in quotation marks. "When I saw you standing on the steps in front of that house with the wind blowing your hair, looking so anxious, in that suit… I remember the color…"

"You thought, Gosh, I want to marry her and keep her forever?"

"I thought, God, I want to get in her pants…"

I began to giggle, and Martin's hand came out of the darkness and stroked my cheek.

"Good night," he said, on the edge of sleep. "You have never disappointed me."

"Good night," I answered, and let go of the day.

My little traveling clock on the night table told me it was seven-thirty, and the wailing from next door told me Hayden had started his cycle.

I hopped out of bed before I was fully awake, and the cold of the floor gave me a nasty shock. Our house in Lawrenceton had hardwood floors too, but they never felt this cold. I slid my feet into slippers as I headed for the door, and I crossed over to the "nursery" with the soles slapping the floor pleasantly. The house seemed very quiet except for Hayden, who was red faced and sobbing when I got to him.

He'd slept all night.

"Mama's here," I said, my voice still thick with sleep. "Don't cry, baby!" I scooped him up from the crib, after figuring out how to lower the side. I only knew cribs had sides that lowered because I'd watched my friend Lizanne do the honors on her baby's bed. For mothers less than five feet tall, the lowered side was an essential feature. Not that I was a mother! I warned myself, catching my error.

"Heat a bottle, please, Martin?" I called down the stairs as I changed Hayden on our bed. He definitely didn't like the cold air smacking his damp bottom, and I didn't blame him. He was overdue for a sponge bath, but I dreaded giving him one in this chilly house.

Down the stairs we went, Hayden still complaining but not as frantically.

The kitchen was empty. Far from coffee waiting for me

and a bottle awaiting Hayden, everything looked boringly like it had the night before.

The door to the back porch opened. Martin stepped in, stamping his feet, and stood on a little rug by the back door to take off his boots. He stepped through to the kitchen in his stocking feet.

"Look outside, Roe!" he said, with the grin of a twelve-year-old.

For the first time I glanced out of the windows; and I realized why the house had seemed so silent. The fields and the driveway were covered with snow.

"Oh my God," I said, stunned. I stared at the heavy white coating. "Oh. Wow." From one horizon to the next, it was the same. "I've never seen that much snow in my life."

"I almost wish we had a sled," he said.

"I almost wish I had a cup of coffee."

"Coming right up." Martin was awful damn cheerful. Who could have guessed snow would have that effect? I sat there in a semiconscious lump while Martin heated the baby bottle, started the coffee, and made toast with a beautiful toaster that had to have been a wedding present for Regina and Craig.

Martin even hummed. He is not a hummer.

He took Hayden and gave him his bottle. "Look out there, fella. Snow everywhere! When you get bigger you can bundle up and go out there and make snow angels and pee in the snow and make a snowman . . ."

I sensed a theme.

By the time Martin had wound down, I had had time to pour two cups of coffee down my throat and eat my toast, too.

"Can we get out of here?" I asked. I took my third cup with me to the window. "I mean, can your car get out of the driveway?"

Martin looked serious, all of a sudden. He loves that Mercedes, for sure.

"I'll call Karl," he said, and vanished.

I tried to remember Karl from our wedding, which Martin had assured me Karl attended. I was drawing a blank. Of course, I'd been so nervous I was surprised I'd gotten the responses right.

I occupied myself by spreading towels by the kitchen sink to give Hayden that quick sponge bath I felt obliged to give him. He hated it just as much as he had the last time I'd tried this process, maybe even objecting more loudly because it was so cold. I'd already had dark doubts about this little ritual, which Amina had assured me was obligatory. After all, how dirty could Hayden get? I cleaned his bottom every time I changed him.

But I dutifully soaped the hands that never grasped food and the feet that never took a step. At least, I told myself bracingly, all this complaining would surely wear out the baby, resulting in a good nap.

"Karl's coming out," Martin told me.

"Great. Remind me about Karl?"

"Karl Bagosian, whose family was Armenian a couple of generations ago. He went to school with me, though he's a couple of years older."

"So what does Karl do now?"

"He owns the Jeep place."

I nodded wisely. It was all becoming clear.

"So you fellas were buddies through school?"

Martin shrugged. "Yeah, we were. We were on the football team together. We went hunting together. He dated Barby for a while. We joined the army together."

"Speaking of high school buddies, what's the story on Dennis Stinson?"

"I always hated that son of a bitch," my husband said, with very little change in his voice.

"He seemed nice to me." I tried to look innocent. "Just because he's moved in on your ex-wife..."

"Cindy and I have been divorced for a long time," Martin said. "I don't think it's that... or maybe, not much. And he tried to copy off my paper in geometry." I couldn't help it, I started laughing. Martin had the grace to look abashed. "Dennis just... I wouldn't have minded Cindy living with someone, if it had been Karl. But Karl went and got himself married to a girl that just got out of college, right about the same time you and I got married. He's got kids older than her, I think."

If the amazing Karl was going to bring us a Jeep, I needed to get dressed. Jeans, a sweater, and boots seemed to be the uniform of the day, judging by Martin, who seemed to be more relaxed than he'd been in days. He even laid Hayden in the middle of our bed and brushed my hair for me, a pleasant pastime we hadn't had a chance to indulge in lately.

Since Hayden remained content, I called my mother, but missed her both at her house and at the hospital. I left a message on her answering machine, and talked to John's oldest son at the hospital. He said his father was on the upswing, that they hoped to take him home the next day, and he knew my mother would want to tell me all the details. He further informed me that my mother was holding up just fine, which I hadn't doubted for a second.

Next I called Angel and Shelby to ask about the baby, found out little Joan was perfect in every respect, and Angel was recovering from the birth in record time.

I handed the phone to Martin so he could call the Pan-Am Agra plant, but he told me he'd already talked to his second-in-command that morning. I glanced at my watch and winced. If you wanted to work for Martin, you had to get up early and be bright the minute you slid from between your sheets.

"But I do need to talk to David in Receiving," Martin decided. He punched in numbers wearing his business face, so I went downstairs and poured another cup of coffee.

Just then I heard a chugging noise, and looking out the window I saw a bright red Jeep coming through the snow. I could only assume it was on the driveway.

A man hopped out and began slogging his way to the front door.

Karl Bagosian was about Martin's height, maybe five-nine or five-ten. His head was bare, and I saw that his hair was very thick and coarse, and very dark, though graying, an attractive complement to his olive complexion. Martin was still on the phone, so I unlocked the door and threw it open.

"Hello," Karl said, looking up at the sound. He gave me a comprehensive but brief scan, and lowered his eyes to make sure he'd stamped all the snow off his boots. Satisfied, he pulled off the boots and left them by the door, padding farther into the living room unselfconsciously, and I began to see this was the protocol in snow country.

"I'm Aurora. Thank you for bringing the Jeep. Martin says he's known you forever."

"Just about." Karl had finished divesting himself of several layers of outerwear and finally looked me in the eyes.

Karl Bagosian had the most beautiful eyes I'd ever seen on a man. On anyone. Large, oval, very dark, fringed by eyelashes most women could only dream of, those eyes could speak to you long enough to talk you right out of your clothes and into Karl's bed.

"Well, I feel like a female peacock," I said, mildly disgruntled. "Would you like some coffee?"

"Yes, please," he said, after a surprised hesitation. Karl preceded me to the kitchen, and I had to remind myself he'd been here many times before . . . before I was born, no doubt. Karl had thickened a little with middle age, and he had white teeth that gleamed like an actor's. He sat at the kitchen table watching me, while I poured a mug of coffee and placed it before him, with milk and sugar handy.

"If you haven't had breakfast, I would be glad to make you some toast," I offered. "Martin's on the phone; he'll be down in just a minute."

"This is southern hospitality, the kind I keep hearing about, I guess."

"It's just hospitality. How else would I treat you?"

He had no answer for that. "This is some mess about Regina, huh?" he asked, looking up at me with those gorgeous eyes. He poured sugar in his coffee with a liberal hand. I watched in amazement as he did the same with the milk. It hardly looked like coffee anymore.

I propped myself against the kitchen counter. "Did you know Craig?"

"Yeah, he stole a car from my lot."

"What did you do?"

"I went after him and got it back." And the large dark eyes didn't look so gorgeous anymore. In fact, they looked downright scary. I realized I was very glad I hadn't been there when Karl had gotten his car back.

"Mr. Vigilante," Martin said from the doorway. He meant to be smiling when he said it, but the smile came off lame. He'd heard the whole conversation.

Karl got up and shook Martin's hand, and they did the shoulder-patting ritual. Deep affection.

"The little sumbitch—'scuse me, Aurora—is just lucky I didn't fix his wagon for good," Karl said, white teeth gleaming. "I only laid off because he was your niece's husband."

"This was since they got married?"

"Yeah, in fact this was last week. Right before he showed up on your doorstep down in Georgia, dead. Maybe he wanted to drive down in a jeep."

"The police know about this?"

"Yeah, I told 'em after I heard Craig got killed. Told 'em I had a key to the house here. They come out here to take a gander."

Karl Bagosian looked so exotic I found I had expected him to have a foreign accent. It was a little shocking to hear a homely midwestern voice coming from his mouth. I thought of him in harem pants. I clamped my lips together.

"What are you smiling about?" Martin asked from my elbow. I jumped.

"Would you like some more coffee, honey?" I asked.

"Lord, she's no bigger than a flea, Martin."

I particularly dislike to be talked about as if I weren't there. But this was Martin's friend.

"Small but mean," Martin said. I looked up, startled, and he was smiling... Lucky for him.

"Was the house very different than it is now? When you brought the police out here?" I asked Karl.

He took a swallow of coffee, raised the cup to me in appreciation. Since Martin had made it, that compliment wasn't due me, but I nodded anyway.

"Yes, the house was a mess," Karl said bluntly. "All I did was hang up the clothes and vacuum, run the dishwasher. That made a big difference."

"Thank you," I said, impressed at his enterprise. "Did the police seem to think anything had happened here in the house?"

"It was just like they'd gone shopping," Karl said, shaking his head. "Like they were both going to be back any moment. Oh, I forgot to empty the waste-baskets that day, I just recalled. Sorry. Darlene was with me, but that girl is bone lazy."

"How old is Darlene now?" Martin pulled out a chair, settled in opposite his friend.

"She's twenty-six."

Martin was seriously shocked. "Not... your daughter Darlene? Is twenty-six?"

Karl nodded. "And she's my youngest. Darlene is responsible for every one of these gray hairs."

"How old are your others, now?" Martin sounded apprehensive.

Karl cast his eyes up, as if the answer would be written on the high ceiling. "Lessee. Gil is thirty, 'bout to be thirty-one. Therese is twenty-nine."

Martin looked at me, horrified. I shrugged, smiling. The difference in our ages had always bothered Martin more than me. Martin, who worked out and played killer racquetball, had always had the body of a younger man. Not that my experience was that broad... but he'd always pleased me, and he knew it. As far as mental attitudes went, Martin and I had our differences, but no more than any two people have.

"How old are you, Aurora? Martin's looking worried." Karl was not a man who would miss much. "My wife, Phoebe, is just a kid, too; she's twenty-five."

"I'm older than your wife *and* your children." I gestured toward his mug, asking if he wanted a refill.

"No, thanks," Karl said. "Martin, you ready to run me back into town?"

"Thanks for bringing the Jeep out, Karl," I said. I perceived that it was *mano a mano* time, and I was being left behind.

"Do you need me to get anything while I'm in town, Roe?" Martin was already putting on his coat and sliding the cell phone into his pocket. I sighed, but tried to keep it silent. Tracking down a scrap of paper took a minute, but I quickly made a list of things we'd neglected to get the day before.

In the back of my mind was the fear the snow would get worse, and we'd be marooned out here. What if we lost our heat?

What if whoever had killed Craig came here looking for Regina?

This was a thought so sudden and shocking that I really regretted having it, especially since I was watching the bright red Jeep recede down the driveway with Martin and Karl inside when the idea came to full bloom in my mind.

I paced around the house distractedly, trying to rid myself of the fear. It hardly made sense that whoever killed Craig in Georgia would come looking here—and that was assuming the killer hadn't been Regina herself. I managed to talk myself out of the worst of my funk, but a quarter of an hour later I was still padding around the house in two pairs of socks; staring out the windows at the snow.

After checking on the now-napping Hayden, I pulled on my boots and stuffed the baby monitor in my coat pocket. Gloved and hatted, I stepped out the south-facing front door and watched my boots sink into the snow.

I'd seen ice, I'd seen sleet, and one memorable January we'd had three inches of snow and been out of school for two and a half days. But I'd never in my life seen white stuff this deep, probably six to eight inches. I knew from what Martin had said about his childhood that it was likely this snow wouldn't melt for weeks, but only be deepened by subsequent storms.

The sky was an oppressive leaden gray, just like yesterday. It seemed quite probable to me that—amazing though the thought was—it was going to snow again. If we'd been on a vacation in a ski lodge, with lots of fireplaces and smiling servers, that would've been one thing. But out here in Farm Country, with the fireplace in the living room that at least also served our bedroom upstairs, we'd have to do a lot of fetching and carrying if our electricity went out. The other rooms would be icy. I made a mental note to use the stove to prepare as many bottles of formula as I could while I had the wherewithal.

Since I wanted to stay close enough for the monitor to work, I'd been tramping around the house in a circle. I'd noted with relief that there was a woodpile in the western side yard, the one farthest from the road, and I'd even brushed some of the snow off the wood to check that the pile was as large as it seemed.

But as I prepared to slog off and finish my circuit, I spied something I hadn't noticed earlier. There were other footprints in the snow, prints that had been made some time in the night, since they were half filled in. Though it was a little hard to tell the heel end from the toe end, there was no mistaking these prints for deer tracks, or the trail of any other kind of wildlife.

Feeling like Hawkeye, I visually followed the marks. The prints approached the front-facing kitchen window from the south, across the fields, and then circled the house; just like my path, but closer to the windows, so the owner of the prints could look into the rooms.

Or maybe the steps left and returned? But that was crazy. Why would Martin climb out the window to leave the house? He'd entered at the back porch door this morning. I could see his tracks, still crisp and clear, and I recognized the tread of his boots. He'd come out that back door, tromped over to an oak tree, walked even farther west away from the road, rotated in a tight circle to take in the view, and made his way back to the same door.

I swallowed the lump of fear in my throat.

Someone else had been lurking around the farmhouse. I tried like hell to think of another reasonable—or even unreasonable—explanation, but I could think of none, not a single damn one.

The snow had done such a great job of cheering up Martin that I hated to deflate his balloon. But I decided I had to tell him about the tracks. I cut short my expedition and stomped my boots on the back steps as Martin had done, leaving mine on the little rug where his had rested earlier, right inside the door. On the kitchen counter close to the dining table, Martin had left the little Corinth phone book open to the yellow pages (Car Dealerships) and I spared a moment to be deeply thankful that Regina and Craig had had phone service.

The man who answered agreed to go see if Karl and Martin had made it into town yet.

"Yes?" Martin asked crisply, after a lengthy pause. He was using his business voice.

"Martin, someone was outside during the night," I told him.

This was what I loved about Martin. He didn't say, "Are you sure?" or "That's ridiculous!" He asked, "How did you find out?"

After I described the footprints and my line of reasoning, there was another appreciable pause.

"I guess the light wasn't good enough this morning for me to notice the tracks. You're locked up now?" he asked.

"Yes."

"Baby asleep?"

"Yes."

"Then go upstairs, look in my suitcase, and get out the gun."

"Okay." Jeez, I hated guns. But I was scared enough to listen.

"It's loaded. You remember how I showed you how to take off the safety, how to fire?"

"Yes."

"If the footprints are blurry, there's nothing to worry about. Whoever made them is long gone. But just in case, it would be good if you had the gun handy. Wouldn't it make you feel better?"

"I guess so."

"Okay, now. You call the woman who was over last night, Margaret what's-her-name, see if she can come stay with you. I'm going to do a couple things here in town and then I'll be right back out."

"Okay." What could he have to do in town? Maybe Martin had thought of something to improve the farm's security. What we needed out here was a large ferocious barking dog, I decided.

After a few more exchanges, we hung up. I high-tailed it up the stairs and rummaged through Martin's suitcase for his automatic. I hated to even touch the thing, but stronger than that loathing was the desire to protect myself and the baby in this Ohio farmhouse.

8

Thirty minutes later, I was feeling much more secure. Martin's Ruger was near at hand but not obvious, stashed in an otherwise empty drawer in the kitchen, and Margaret Granberry, who'd been glad to come over, was having a cup of coffee at the kitchen table. She was also holding Hayden, who of course had woken up just as I was saying hello to Margaret.

I was ready to take him from her to give him his bottle.

"I'll do it," she volunteered.

Oddly enough, I almost told her no. No, to the first offer of help I'd had with this baby. I had actually opened my mouth to demur, to say that I was used to it, to protest that this was my job.

I forced myself to smile and say, "Here."

Margaret pushed the coffee cup all the way across the table so she wouldn't spill hot liquid on the baby by some accident, and took Hayden gently in her arms. I'd shaken the bottle and tested the formula, so I handed it to her and she began to feed him.

"Have you had children yourself?" I asked, relaxing when it was evident the baby was fine.

She shook her head. "Nope. I don't want to give you

more of our history than you want, but Luke and I have been married for ten years. The first few years, we could afford hospitalization insurance, so getting fertility testing was just out of the question. About three years ago, Luke's mom passed away, and she left her money in a trust fund for us. But by that time... I'm quite a bit older than Luke, and though we went on with the fertility testing, we didn't have much hope. Rightly, as it turned out."

Almost happy to have company in my predicament, since it made me feel not so inadequate, I told Margaret. "I'm not fertile, either." When she seemed interested, I told her about my unpleasant experiences with a top gynecologist in Atlanta, and Martin's indifference to our having our own baby. Suddenly I realized how much I was saying, and I apologized. "I don't like to talk about my reproduction problems at home," I said wryly. "It's like people know I failed, and they look at you like you're lacking something. Getting pregnant is so easy for so many women."

Margaret shifted Hayden slightly, held up the bottle to see how much was left. Hayden protested, and she smiled and slid the nipple back into his mouth. "Luke can't understand how women can talk about something as personal as fertility problems," Margaret said. The cold sun lit her red hair until it almost seemed to give off warmth. "It does seem strange to think that in this day and age there are some medical problems beyond fixing."

"I know," I agreed fervently. "You keep thinking that this can't be an end of it, there must be something else they can do. If they can accomplish so much in other fields, why can't they fix you so you can have a baby?"

"Martin was married before, right? To the Cindy who runs the flower shop?"

"Martin has a grown son. You might not know if you haven't been living in Corinth that long, but Barrett's an actor. He's got a recurring guest spot on one of those nighttime soap operas. That's why I think Martin had a kind of 'been there, done that,' attitude about having another baby."

Margaret nodded. "It's snowing again," she observed, glancing out the curtainless window before turning her attention back to Hayden.

"I'm ready for Martin to get back. I live in the country at home, but somehow the snow makes this place feel even more isolated," I confessed, thinking I sounded pretty whiney and should probably shut my mouth. Growing up in the same general area, maybe Margaret was accustomed to the deafening silence of the snowfall. Had it been very lonely for her out here? "Did you see Craig and Regina much?" I asked.

"Not at first," she answered, after a moment. "We're so much older, and they were newlyweds. And Luke and I are both busy. But they got bored playing house after a while, and then we saw them more and more."

"What did you think of the marriage?"

"That's a big question." Margaret Granberry hunched her head to her shoulder to push her flaming hair back behind her ear while she continued to feed the baby. "Were—are—you and Regina close?"

"No. I hardly know her."

"In that case… I'll tell you, I never could quite figure out why Regina and Craig got married. Their friend Rory was here all the time, and between you and me, I think there was something of a ménage à trois going on . . . strange though that is to think of in Ohio farming country!" She laughed, and I tried to politely join in.

Margaret noticed my lack of enthusiasm. "I'm sorry," she said, a smile belying her contrite words. "We tried that Missionary Bible Church last weekend, and the people there were so fire-and-brimstone, the contrast with our lovebirds out here was really sharp."

"Martin's parents went to that church," I said. "At least, his stepfather made Martin and Barby go after he married their mother. They had a terrible experience there."

"I heard about it from one of the women in my book readers' club," Margaret said. "His sister Barbara, Barby? She got pregnant, right? And they drove her out. I hope you don't mind me bringing it up. It's a famous piece of local history."

"That was after Martin's mother died, and Barby was just sixteen or fifteen, very young. Isn't it just bitter, when you can't conceive, how easily other women can?" I made myself drop that line of whine. "Martin's stepdad got up in front of the church and denounced Barby and asked the congregation to pray for her."

"What happened?" Margaret's light eyes were bright with interest.

"Martin punched out his stepfather," I admitted. "Then he joined the army."

"What happened to his sister?"

"She was put in a home for unwed mothers, I believe." When Martin told me the story, and it was one he hated to remember, it was because he was explaining why his family farm was in the hands of a man who hated him.

"You don't know the rest of the story?"

"No. Martin was hazy on that part because he had left for boot camp. I never had the nerve to ask Barby. She and I aren't good friends. Besides which, I know that had to have been terribly painful."

"Giving up your baby? I can't imagine that."

"But then, what kind of childhood would that baby have had in a household run by Joseph Flocken? Mothered by a sixteen-year-old?"

"Good points. Ones I should've considered, since my own husband was an adopted child. His parents were just great."

"I'm glad for him. It must be a consolation, to know you were wanted enough to be selected over others."

Margaret shrugged.

"Where do you think the footprints lead?" I asked, standing up to look out the side window. I hadn't wanted to frighten Margaret, but it would have been wrong to ask her to come over because I was anxious without telling her why.

"Unless they go across the fields all the way to our farm, I think they'll end in that little grove of trees in that hollow," she said. She'd gotten up with Hayden propped upright on her shoulder, and she was patting him so he'd burp.

"Why?"

"Because that's the only place big enough to hide a truck or car," Margaret said practically.

I hadn't thought about it, but if a prowler didn't want to freeze his booty off, he'd have to have come in a vehicle, and that vehicle would have had to be parked somewhere unobtrusive. My neighbor was right.

"So how did the car, if there was one, get to the grove?"

"There's a little turnoff from the highway there, and a dirt lane runs between the fields."

"Oh," I said lamely. Margaret knew her local geography. "Is that your land?"

"That's the boundary between the farms. Regina would walk from there and back to the house every day. I guess she was exercising because she was pregnant."

"And you really didn't suspect?"

Margaret looked embarrassed. "I never said I didn't know, exactly. I guess I did think she was expecting. But I had no idea she was as far along as she was." Margaret wrinkled her classic nose. "I guess now... I should have asked her about it. But I didn't think it was any of my business. The past three months, I didn't see her to talk to that often. Where shall I put the baby?" Hayden had fallen asleep.

"I'll carry him up." Margaret eased the baby over to me, and I carefully navigated the stairs with his heavy little body clutched to my chest. My guest had helped herself to another cup of coffee by the time I came back down. She was looking out the window of the living room, and I joined her. The Granberrys' dark green Dodge pickup was parked to one side of the front door, and we stood side by side contemplating it. Margaret was about eight inches taller than I, and broad shouldered, but there was an air of feyness, of frailty, about her.

"I just can't understand why Regina wouldn't tell everyone she was pregnant," Margaret said, her head moving gently from side to side in an amazed negative.

According to Margaret, Regina *had* been pregnant... so if the baby I was calling Hayden was indeed Regina's child, he hadn't been kidnapped, and at least that was a crime I could wipe off Regina's slate in my mind.

"Why indeed," I murmured, mostly to myself. The only reason I could think of... Oh, ew, no. I winced.

"You had a thought?" Margaret asked. "You look like you just ate a lemon."

"What if she didn't plan to keep the baby?"

"You mean, give it up for adoption?"

"Maybe. But I was thinking..." I just hated to voice the thought, and I couldn't even formulate why I found it so loathsome.

Margaret was looking down at me expectantly. "What?"

"What if she was carrying the baby for someone else?"

"You mean, got pregnant on purpose? On commission, like?"

"Or got inseminated with someone else's sperm, so the baby would be the true child of half the couple." At least Margaret seemed to be able to follow my sometimes fractured thinking process. She was nodding.

"You may have something there, Aurora," she said. "But I find it makes me think much less of Regina, that she would exploit someone's infertility for her own support."

She began to clear the few dishes off the table, and I began running hot water to wash them. As we washed, rinsed, and dried, Margaret told me about an art exhibit she and Luke had driven into Pittsburgh to see the week before, but I was still thinking about Regina.

9

The surrogate-mother theory explained a great deal. Why Regina had stayed out of sight while she was pregnant. She wouldn't have wanted to answer a lot of questions.

Why she had money in the diaper bag. She would have been paid for her pregnancy, and presumably she would've received money for expenses during it. That would be why she and Craig had been able to afford to live without government aid, even though neither she nor Craig held a steady job.

"I'd been thinking," I said slowly, "that Craig had gotten involved with some drug deal or some scam of his that had gone wrong. But that didn't explain all the facts."

Margaret shrugged. "I've had a month or two to wonder about it. Regina's attitude seemed so strange."

"But why would someone kill Craig? And take Regina?"

"Maybe nobody took Regina. Maybe she went."

"Leaving her baby?"

"People leave babies all the time," Margaret said, her face grim. "Luke and I lived in Pittsburgh before we moved back here so Luke could help his mother out during her last illness. The first year we were married, before we were trying to have our own child, this woman in our apartment building left her baby right outside our door. She was thinking since we didn't have kids, we would be ecstatic, I guess."

"Oh my gosh! What did you do?"

"Of course we called the police, and they called the child welfare people. They had to take the baby to a foster home."

"That's so sad! What happened to the mother?"

Margaret shrugged. "Jail time, I think."

It had certainly become a morning of mysteries to ponder. Why a woman would have a baby she didn't want... why she'd leave that baby's life to chance... and where was the father of the baby, all this time, huh? Why did his responsibility get to be voluntary, while the mother's was mandatory? I thought of my father, who'd never sent child support; Regina's father, who had vanished the minute the divorce was final.

Boy, in a minute I was going to be spitting fire because I wasn't allowed in combat. I shook myself briskly and asked Margaret Granberry if she'd seen the latest Harrison Ford movie.

Our husbands lurched up the driveway in their separate vehicles. We had quite a convention in front of the house now, with Margaret's dark green pickup, Martin's (leased, rented, or borrowed) Jeep, and Luke's battered sort-of-white Bronco.

Luke hopped out of the Bronco and hurried to the front door, his face reddened by the cold. He was wearing a rugged coat that looked like sheepskin or some other animal hide, and he'd gone without a hat or gloves. Martin, who hated headgear—I suspected because it messed up his hair—was impressed enough by the cold to have put on a sort of Russian hat he'd had for years, and he'd worn the leather driving gloves I'd given him last Christmas. His arms were full of bags from the grocery.

"I got your message," Luke told Margaret breathlessly. "Is everything okay here?"

"Yes, honey," she said. "I didn't mean to scare you. I left Luke a note about why I'd come over here," she explained to me in an aside. "I didn't want Luke to think I'd just ducked out on the firewood we were supposed to split this morning!"

"Oh, I'm so sorry I interrupted your chores!" I had assumed that because it had snowed, everyone was on holiday, I realized. A legacy of my southern upbringing.

"No, no. We can just as well do it this afternoon. I've enjoyed the break in routine."

Luke said to Martin, "My wife tells me you've had a prowler."

"You wouldn't think this was the weather for it, would you?"

"Mighty brave guy," Luke commented, in agreement.

"Or desperate."

Martin went to put the groceries in the kitchen, leaving this little chilling statement hanging in the air behind him like an icicle from the eaves.

I smiled at the Granberrys, but I felt it was an anxious sort of smile. "I'll go see if we can find some hot chocolate," I murmured, and scooted into the kitchen after Martin.

"What are you in such a snit about?" I breathed at him.

He was standing in his "I'm mad" pose, shoulders hunched up, hands in his pockets, staring out the window.

"I can't track down that slippery little bastard," Martin growled back. I assumed he meant Rory Brown.

I started to point out that this was no big surprise, but my better sense came to my rescue. "We'll talk about it later. Let's serve the Granberrys some hot chocolate. After all, they came to help when we needed it."

Martin carried the tray with the four mugs out to the living room and set it on the battered table in front of the couch. The tray was clearly one of Regina and Craig's wedding presents, probably from Pier 1, a rattan and iron construction that would have looked charming in more congruent surroundings.

"Do you have any idea how long you'll stay?" Luke asked, taking a mug of chocolate and dropping some miniature marshmallows on top. He seemed like a different person now that he was sure his wife was safe—relaxed and secure, even physically larger somehow.

I let Martin field that one.

"We have no idea," he confessed. "If Regina is found, and under what circumstances . . . if we can track down my sister, Barby, and her fiancé . . . if we can find out if the baby is really Regina's . . . All that will have a bearing."

"What a terrible set of circumstances," Margaret said. She didn't seem inclined to repeat the ideas she'd voiced to me when we were alone, and I thought that was wise. I'd try to tell Martin when the Granberrys left.

Luke was the first to hear yet another vehicle coming up the driveway.

"Expecting anyone?" he asked Martin.

"No." Martin went to the front window. "Blue Dodge pickup."

To my astonishment, our newest set of callers consisted of the hunky Dennis Stinson, Cindy Bartell, and our erstwhile trip companion, Rory.

This house *had* seemed isolated. Now it was beginning to feel like a social center. We should have charged for parking and hot beverages. I went to the kitchen to put some more water in the pot, found some cookies in the bags Martin had carried into the house, and put them on a plate.

"The shop's closed on Saturday afternoons, so we thought we'd come out to check on you," Dennis said. He looked even larger in the layers of cold-weather wear. Cindy looked like one of Santa's elves next to him, with her pixie-cut hair and narrow face. She was in a red-and-green sweater, which heightened the impression. Rory wasn't smiling, or even wearing his usual look of amiable stupidity. On the contrary, he seemed sullen and stubborn. He didn't speak, but grabbed a cookie and ate it in one bite.

I sidled over next to him, since all the other people in the room were talking to each other and I had a little time on my own.

"How come you're here?"

"That Stinson guy grabbed me," Rory said. He looked down at me, ran his tongue around his teeth to clean off the cookie remnants, and summoned back up his charm. "I oughta call the police," he said, all naughty. "I was just walking around downtown, minding my own business. Then I cross in front of Cindy's Flowers and out comes this Stinson guy, and he grabs me and tells me your husband is looking for me and I gotta go with him. Then Mrs. Bartell, she says I got to go, too. Since it was her, I came without giving them no trouble."

"Thanks, Rory. We really do need to find out more about what happened to Craig and why."

"I told you everything I know!"

"That's hard to believe," I told him, surprised at my own directness. "You were living out here with Craig and Regina, weren't you? Isn't that your stuff up there, in one of the extra bedrooms?"

Rory gave me a fleeting look: bright eyed, hard. "What we did here isn't any of your business," he told me, with some justification.

"Don't speak to my wife like that," Martin said coldly. He had appeared by my side with his usual silence. "We don't care about your love life. We just want to find out where Regina is, and whose baby this is."

"Whose?" Rory looked down at his feet. He didn't seem to understand what Martin meant, and I thought, That could mean two things. "Well, as long as that baby is here, anyone could claim it, couldn't they? Anyone could say anything about that baby, who's gonna say no? Nobody knows nothing except me."

That was a real conversation stopper, and it got the attention of almost everyone in the room.

The silence was broken by Karl Bagosian's entrance through the kitchen porch. I was so surprised to see him, I involuntarily said, "Where'd you come from, Karl?" Then, shaking my head at my own rudeness, I said, "Excuse me! It's good to see you again so soon! Would you like some coffee or hot chocolate?" I registered the fact that Karl wasn't wearing his prosperous midwestern car-salesman clothing anymore, but some very practical cold-weather wear.

Karl was looking at Rory Brown with the coldest, most assessing look I'd ever seen. If I'd been on the receiving end of it, I'd have been as silent as Rory, and just as scared.

"Hey, Mr. Bagosian," Rory said finally. "How you doing? How's Therese?"

"Don't speak her name." How theatrical the words sounded, and yet none of us even thought of laughing. Karl was deadly serious.

Therese? I searched around the corners of my brain, finally remembered Therese was Karl's middle child.

"I need to talk to you for a minute, Martin," Karl said. "In the kitchen."

Talk about your social challenges.

"Rory," I said brightly, "wouldn't you like to go upstairs and gather your things together? Then you wouldn't have to make another trip out here!"

To my relief, he took the verbal shove and went up the steps. Somehow, Rory looked much more at home in the house than I did. I fetched a baggy old sweater with big pockets I'd draped over the back of one of the kitchen chairs. Karl and Martin were deep in conversation, so I didn't speak to them. I'd had the sweater on under my coat this morning when I'd gone out in the snow and seen the tracks, and the nursery monitor was still in the left-hand pocket.

I glanced back through the doorway at our uninvited guests, who took the hint and began making small talk. Hayden, who'd been up for a few minutes, had been deposited in his infant seat by Martin, and of course he came in for a share of the conversation. The nightfall of snow was another hot topic, and after that, odds and ends of town gossip that were as boring to me as Lawrenceton gossip would be to any of these people. I was able to gather from the snips I caught as I refreshed mugs and fetched napkins that Margaret had once been a schoolteacher, Dennis Stinson supported the Dallas Cowboys, and more snow was expected today.

The hoot of a horn attracted my attention, and I went to the front door to see an old black pickup with an attachable sign that said U.S. MAIL sitting on the roof. The mail carrier was leaning out of the passenger window, a box and some envelopes in her hand.

"Hello," I called, and stepped out with only my sweater for warmth. The receiver for the nursery monitor, stuffed down in one of the big pockets, banged as I walked. I was glad I had my boots on. I crossed my arms over my chest as the breathtaking cold dove into my lungs.

"You the new people?" the woman asked. She was round all over and had a very misguided haircut, kind of a poorly done old-fashioned shag. She reeked of cigarette smoke.

"We're staying here temporarily. We're the owners," I said, close enough to the windows to lower my voice. The chug of the engine was loud in the snow-induced hush.

"Just wanted to check. I have a package here for the renter. You want to accept it? You want me to hold it until she comes back?"

It was a box from Victoria's Secret. Good Lord.

"I'll keep it for her," I said reluctantly, and tucked the box under my arm. The mail carrier had thoughtfully put a rubber band around the package to hold the envelopes to it.

"What's your name?" the carrier bellowed.

"Teagarden, and my husband's name is Bartell, but I don't think we'll be getting any mail here," I explained. "Do you just leave it in the mailbox out by the road?"

"Yes, normally, but this box wouldn't fit, and when I saw tracks going in, I thought I could be sure someone would be up here," she said. "Well, nice to meetcha."

I thanked her, and clutching the package across my chest and shivering, the heavy pocket of my sweater banging against my stomach, I darted back into the house.

"That was Geraldine Clooney," Margaret said with some amusement. "What did you think?"

"She's one of a kind," I said.

Cindy and Dennis laughed. Luke wasn't in the room. Karl was pouring himself another cup of coffee, and Martin was coming down the stairs. The baby wasn't in his infant seat. Martin must have put him in his crib.

I wondered why Rory hadn't come down with his things.

I wondered what Karl and Martin had been talking about in the kitchen.

I wondered at the officiousness of Dennis and Cindy. Telling Rory that we wanted to see him was one thing; bundling him up and practically kidnapping him was another. If Dylan or Karl had brought Rory out, I wouldn't have wondered, but Cindy and Dennis?

As often happens to me, my mind began drifting along its own path. There's nothing like being alone in a crowd to spark a really interesting little thought pattern. I wondered how the Corinthians dug graves in the snow. Did the ground actually freeze, like the tundra? Would I get to see a snowplow? Did snow-plows clean driveways, too?

"Roe? Roe?"

"Yes?" I gasped.

"I'm sorry," Margaret said, concern in her voice. "But I was telling you that we were going to be going now. You seemed so out of it."

"Just daydreaming, I'm afraid," I said, trying to sound matter-of-fact. "Thank you so much for coming to my rescue this morning."

"I think I left my purse in the kitchen."

"Of course, let me go get it." I scooted into the kitchen. There was a rifle leaning against the wall by the back porch door. I absorbed all of this in one comprehensive glance, snatched up Margaret's purse from the counter, and handed it to her in the living room within seconds.

"I don't see Karl's transportation out there, Aurora," Margaret said. I looked up at her and shrugged.

"You got me," I said cheerfully. "Men are strange."

Amusement crossed the pale face. "Come see me," she said warmly, and waving good-bye to the others, she and her husband made their way through the rutted snow to their vehicles.

Well, that was two fewer things blocking the view down to the little copse. I was loading the tray with used cups when I heard a strange little rustling sound. The oddest thing about it was that the sound seemed to be issuing from my appendix.

I thought about it as I carried the tray to the kitchen, sliding it carefully onto the counter. I looked down anxiously, I admit, and felt like a total idiot when I realized the sound had been issuing from the nursery monitor. Hayden must be moving around in the crib, I figured.

But . . . rustling? Karl came in just then, politely bringing an empty Equal packet. He looked around, spied the trash can, and dropped in the bit of paper. Since he was a courteous and orderly person, he tried not to ask me what I was doing staring at a nursery monitor as if it were communicating with me, but since he was also the man who'd been outside toting a rifle, he had to ask. Picking up on my concentration, he simply pointed a finger and raised his eyebrows inquiringly.

"Listen," I whispered, as if the receiver could also be broadcasting what I said. I held it up to his ear. Karl's dark face looked puzzled. The rustling had been succeeded by a series of baffling little noises, a little *whump*, a small rattling sound, the unmistakable tiny noises of a baby fussing in his sleep. Then footsteps, getting a little fainter.

"Eh!" said Hayden, so I knew he was all right. Following the sound of the footsteps, I looked out of the kitchen across the living room to the stairs, down which Rory Brown came, carrying his backpack and a paper bag full of clothes.

"He took something out of Hayden's room," I said. I was across the rooms and up the stairs before I knew what I was doing, and passed Rory without so much as looking at him.

Hayden was still asleep, restlessly, and the sheet on his crib mattress had been taken off and then replaced. Since it had been a regular flat bedsheet, much folded to fit the crib mattress, I'd noticed how it'd been tucked before, and I knew that it had been removed and refolded. The receiving blanket I'd covered the sheet with had been placed back on top, but it was wrinkled and crooked. As long as Hayden was all right, I couldn't see that any harm had been done, but I was mighty puzzled.

When I came slowly down to the living room, I saw that Cindy and Dennis were about to go.

"Rory's going to stay here for a while," Martin was saying, smilingly. "I'll get him back into town."

Cindy looked doubtful. "Are you sure, Martin? It looks like it's going to let go any minute." The sky looked heavy with snow, the fields and the sky blending into one big sheet of dirty white. Dennis, his hand holding Cindy's, was looking over his shoulder at the horizon, and he was clearly anxious to be gone.

"C'mon, Cindy, we'll see Martin later," he said. "And thank you, Aurora, for the coffee. You'll have to tell Cindy how you do it. Her coffee is not her strong point."

I thought of barfing all over his boots, but decided that was a little extreme. Cindy was red. I met her eyes, and elaborately drew my finger across my throat and made a choking noise. She laughed, a little reluctantly, but laughed. This confused Dennis—of course, it would.

"See you!" Martin called from the kitchen, where he and Rory and Karl were standing in a somewhat strained grouping.

"Good-bye," I said brightly, ready for them all to be gone. Something was fishy, and the sooner Dennis and Cindy pulled away, the sooner I'd find out what it was.

10

I went in the kitchen to face what looked like an interrogation. Martin and Karl had taken the paper bag from Rory, and as I entered they dumped it on the table.

I gasped. Besides the usual deodorant and razor, underpants and condoms, the bag contained packages of bills. Just like the one in the baby's diaper bag, the one I'd discovered in Lawrenceton.

"They were under the sheet on the crib," I said, into the silence.

"It's mine," Rory said sullenly. "As long as you can't find Regina, it's mine. She shows up, I share it with her. But we owe some of it to the midwife."

"Where'd it come from?" Martin asked. It was the opening salvo in a long bombardment.

An hour later, no one had gotten anywhere, except me. I'd looked up Bobbye Sunday's address in the telephone book, which covered several small towns in the area. The midwife lived in Bushmill, and she wasn't answering her phone. I'd tried her number several times while Martin and Karl questioned Rory. Rory, who was wily if not intelligent, had made up his mind he wasn't going to tell anyone anything. I felt like I was some kind of civil rights observer, there to make sure Rory wasn't thumped by an increasingly exasperated Martin. Karl seemed to consider this Martin's show, but he contributed to the atmosphere of menace by smoldering at Rory, with some effect.

"I never meant to hurt Therese," the boy blurted out of the blue.

Karl slammed his palm against the kitchen table with explosive force. "I told you never to say her name!" he said. Then he turned to me. "Therese is simple," he said bluntly. "She can cope with life, but just barely. Then this guy shows up, tells her after one date he loves her, gets her knocked up. I have to take Therese for an abortion. Phoebe's young enough to have one of her own if she wants; we don't want to raise Therese's kid, and it's not our job. She can't raise a kid, he can't raise a kid, he doesn't even want to marry her. But he had a fit when she had the abortion, which left her crying for weeks. He had a use for the baby, but not for Therese, who hasn't seen or heard from him since."

I looked at Rory in a new light. Rather than a passive accomplice to a plot not yet determined, he was an instigator of a subsidiary plot. Not a very efficient instigator, since Therese's father had taken care of the situation, and would have outfaced Rory under any circumstances...

I was sick of trying to figure out what had happened in this farmhouse in the past few months.

"I'm going to take a ride," I said abruptly.

"You're going to drive in this snow?" My husband looked amazed, and that was all it took to make me grab my coat. I'd been dragged along on this, outvoted by my husband as to the wisdom of bringing Rory back to Corinth, stuck with the care of Hayden, forced to consort with Martin's ex-wife. I was in a royal snit compounded of grievance and self-pity.

"Yes, I am," I replied briefly.

Even as my better sense—and I did have some—told me to stay at the farmhouse, I grabbed the keys from the counter and my purse from the table and rode the crest of my snit out to the Jeep. I climbed into it, and switched on the engine.

It would have served me right if the engine had refused to start or I had driven into the fields on my way to the county road, but to my surprise I got to Route 8 just fine. I paused at the end of the driveway for a minute or two, looking at the map I'd yanked out of the glove compartment.

It was the middle of the afternoon, and the sky outside was about to loose its load of snow. I wished I could close my eyes or wiggle my nose and make the kitchenful of men disappear. Then I could go back to the farmhouse without losing face.

But I turned right, on my way to the tiny town of Bushmill.

It was easy, after all, to find Bobbye Sunday's office. It was the little building with the snow all over the blackened and broken roof. The trailer parked behind it didn't look damaged, but the snow around it was unbroken.

I looked out of the foggy window of the Jeep, shivering despite its efficient heating.

The nearest convenience store was manned (and I'm using the word loosely) by an adolescent male with acne and chin-length hair parted down the middle. It was not a flattering style, but I told myself that was just because I was old, and feeling older by the minute.

I smiled as winningly as I could. "Can you tell me what happened at the office down the street?" I asked.

"Which one?" he asked indifferently.

I will not snap, I told myself. I will not snap and snarl. "The burned one," I said gently.

"It burned," he said, smirking at the points he was scoring off the old dame who was at least in her thirties. I wondered if he would think it was as funny if I kicked him in the groin. I took a deep breath. Overreaction.

"When did it burn? Was anyone hurt?"

At least he didn't care why I wanted to know. "I guess it was a couple nights ago," he told me finally. "Someone broke in after midnight, the police figure. Stole some computers and stuff, set a fire. I bet she had some painkillers and stuff in there, someone could sell around here." He smirked again. I felt like giving him a little pain.

"But Miss Sunday is all right?"

"Yep. She was at home when the fire started. She went down there in her nightgown, I heard." Another smirk.

I turned to leave the store, lost in thought.

"Don't you want to buy something?" the boy asked pointedly.

"I do want to find where Bobbye Sunday lives."

"I already told you a lot of stuff," he grumbled. "You need some gas, some cigarettes?"

"No, thank you," I told him, out of all the things I could have said.

It had just dawned on me that I probably knew where Bobbye Sunday lived; the small trailer behind the little office.

The woman that answered my knock was in her early thirties. She was plump and had hair the color of a rusty chrysanthemum. It was either a very inept or a very avant-garde dye job. Either way, it was notable. The cut itself was conventional, short and curly. But her ears were pierced at least four times apiece. Then again she was wearing nurse whites and orthopedic shoes.

Miss Mixed Signals.

"Bobbye Sunday?" I asked.

"Yes." She didn't invite me in, but she didn't bar the door. "Have you come about the fire, are you from the insurance office?"

"No, I'm afraid I'm not." I tried smiling, but she didn't respond. "Could you tell me what happened?"

"Why should I talk to you?" she asked. She slammed the trailer door in my face. Bushmill was chock-full of reticent people.

I trudged back to the Jeep through the snow, feeling my blue jeans brush against my boots with the heavy feel of wet material. My feet were warm and dry, at least, and I made myself stamp the snow out of the treads of my boots before I hoisted myself up into the Jeep.

"Wait!" Bobbye Sunday slogged through the snow, holding her hands out for balance.

"I'm sorry I was so short with you," she said, when she'd reached the side of the Jeep. I'd shut myself in, but rolled down the window. "I lost so much in that fire," the midwife continued. "My patient records, the computers and software I'd just gotten ..."

"I'm sorry," I said. "I'm glad you weren't hurt."

"I keep telling myself that."

"Sometimes that's not much consolation, I guess."

"If you aren't from the insurance company..."

"I just wanted to ask you about a patient you had, a baby you delivered, around three weeks ago? Here, at your office."

"Oh, I can't tell you about that," Bobbye Sunday said firmly. "That's private." She hesitated. "I usually go to the mother's house for delivery, but every now and then I deliver a baby here. That's all I can say."

I could tell she meant it, and I felt sorry for her. "Good-bye," I said, so she could get in out of the cold. "I hope your insurance comes through for you, soon."

She made a face at me, half doubting, half smiling. "Thanks." She turned and made her way through the yard, back to the trailer door.

So that was another door shut.

I found myself wondering about the so-timely fire, destroying the record of Regina's prenatal visits and delivery—if she had indeed delivered in Nurse Sunday's office—right after Rory came back to Corinth. When I thought of Rory's handsome young face, impossibly guileless, I heaved a long sigh. What would we do with Rory? Would he be safe, riding back into Corinth with Karl? Did I care? Would Martin be willing to keep the boy in the house overnight? I wasn't sure I would.

I was grateful to see the entrance to the farm, and even more grateful when I entered the kitchen to find Rory intact and Martin and Karl apparently holding on to their tempers. I tossed down the keys and my purse, realized I'd forgotten to take my boots off at the door, and knelt to dry them with a towel.

"So, what have you guys been talking about?" I asked. I looked up at Karl.

"This fool—" he began, and then the window exploded.

Since I'd been kneeling well away from it, I clearly saw the shards of glass flying into the kitchen, glinting in the fluorescent light. The glass sprayed Rory's left side as he sat slumped at the table, sprayed Martin's right side as he stood across from him, and grazed Karl, who was perched beyond Rory on one corner.

And the bullet that had broken the glass, that bullet hit Rory in the neck on the left side, punching a mortal hole and exiting on the right, causing a shower of blood and tissue that rained on Karl, as the same bullet struck Karl's thigh, hitched over the corner of the table.

At that moment, it seemed, Martin screamed, "Down, down, *down*!" and took a flying leap to land on top of me, flattening me to the floor. A heartbeat later—a heartbeat Rory didn't have—I was facedown on the floor amid the glass and blood, my heart racing at a terrifying pace. Karl was screaming, and Rory bonelessly slid out of his chair and landed two feet away from me, blood pouring out of the wounds in his neck to puddle under him. His eyes were open.

I shrieked without knowing I was going to do it. With Martin weighing me down, I lay shivering and shaking on the floor with Rory's blood spreading toward me.

And then the kitchen was silent.

After the longest minute I'd ever lived through, no more bullets punched through the window. Martin gradually eased off me. I made myself crawl over to Karl, who had begun to moan steadily. The floor was covered with glass, and I found myself thinking of brooms and dustpans—and mops—as the advancing pool of blood stopped inches from me.

"Martin?" I asked hoarsely.

"Yes," he said, breathily.

"Honey, I think Karl has to have a tourniquet."

"Rory?" he asked.

"Dead," I said.

Trying not to sit up, I fumbled my belt out of its loops, and wound it around Karl's thigh. To my intense relief, Martin scooted on his elbows to the other side of the wounded man and drew the belt tight.

Karl became silent, and I risked looking at his face to see he was as pale as his complexion would permit him to get.

I glanced at Martin, wanting to see if Karl's poor condition had registered with him.

I made an incoherent sound of horror. Martin was covered with blood.

My husband, the invincible and strong, the coper with crises.

"Oh, honey," I said. "Oh, honey, you're hurt." Sometimes the obvious truth is the only one that fills your mind and you don't care if you sound smart or not.

"Cuts from the glass," he said briefly. But he was breathing shallowly, and his color was as bad as Karl's.

Without wasting further breath, Martin reached up a cautious hand to get the telephone sitting on the counter.

From upstairs, Hayden began crying. It came over the

monitor clearly. I made as if to rise, and Martin clamped a hand on my shoulder. His grip wasn't strong, but the force of his will was.

"Are you crazy?" he hissed. "Stay down!" He dialed without holding the phone to his ear. I was closer to it, and I could see that the little light, the one that comes on to illuminate the numbers so you can dial in the dark, was off.

"Phone's dead," I told him, unable to control the shaking of my voice. I followed the wire with my eyes, and when it came to the jack, I saw that the phone had not been cut off outside the house, but inside; the little plastic connector had been cut off. I pointed, and Martin followed the line of my finger. For the first time since I'd met him, I saw despair in his eyes.

Martin held it up to his ear to confirm what his eyes had already checked. One of the people who had been our visitors in the past two hours had done this. They'd all been in the kitchen. This was the only phone in the house.

"Where's the cell phone?" I asked.

"It's out in the Jeep."

Of course. I'd seen it there minutes before.

"We'll have to get Karl into the Jeep. We'll call the hospital on our way into town."

"You and the baby have to come." Though he seemed barely conscious, Martin crawled over to the wall and got Karl's rifle.

I couldn't remember how close the Jeep was to the front door. "Let me go check where I parked the Jeep," I told Martin, and crept on my hands and knees to the front door. I stretched up a hand and opened the door, peering around the frame to keep as much of myself covered as possible.

The Jeep was wonderfully close. I felt a surge of hope. We'd get out of here, into town, to the little Corinth hospital.

Then I noticed that the Jeep was canted oddly to one side. My heart did something painful inside my chest when I realized that two of the tires were flat, the two on the side away from the door.

I shut the front door, ran in a crouch to the stairs. They weren't visible from any windows, or at least the angle would be quite acute. I sprinted up as fast as I could, reached the top safely. I stood and panted for a few seconds, trying to get my breathing rate down to something approximately normal, then scurried into Hayden's room, which was over the kitchen. It was safest for him right where he was, I made myself admit, though my every instinct was to pick him up and take him with me. But I couldn't stand the crying. I tried popping his pacifier into his mouth. That would hold him, I hoped.

I didn't want to tell Martin about the Jeep's being disabled, but I had to. He looked even worse than he had three minutes ago, and Karl, I thought, was unconscious.

Martin was still thinking clearly, though.

"Check to see if the phone's still in the Jeep," he told me, though he clearly hadn't much hope. This silent admission that he was not capable of action was more terrifying than anything to me in that horrible kitchen. Martin, strong, dangerous, and brave, had been like a rock at my back for three years. I felt exposed and anguished. "If the phone's not in the Jeep, Karl's pickup is parked behind that clump of trees down in the south field. He went out there to check to see what kind of vehicle whoever was looking in our windows had driven. Then he walked up to the house, following the tracks."

"Okay," I whispered, half distracted by the continuous sound of Hayden's renewed complaining. "So?"

"You'll have to go get Karl's pickup."

"How do we know someone's not out there?" I asked, thinking Martin was nuts. I wasn't about to leave him.

"No more shots," Martin said succinctly.

"Unless they're waiting for us to stand up so they can shoot again," I protested.

"He would've come closer by now and picked us off, if he was still out there. I'm assuming he just wanted Rory."

I glanced over at Karl, whose face was a waxy color I associated with Madame Tussaud's. He was covered with sweat, and blood, and bits of stuff. He looked very bad. Martin had spots of blood on his shirt, mostly on the back where glass slivers had pierced the material as he lay covering me. There was one long cut over his right eye that looked particularly bad, but I reminded myself that head cuts bleed worse than anything. I couldn't give myself any comfort over his color, though, and I knew that something worse than a few cuts was wrong with Martin. I found myself too scared to ask him.

"Take the baby," Martin said.

"What?" This was crazy. It had begun to snow again.

"Take the baby."

"Are you serious?" I said savagely, because I was terrified. "Out in the cold, and I don't know who's out there? I'll drive back here, we'll load Karl in the pickup bed so he can keep his leg stretched out. I'll get the baby then."

"I'm thinking you should drive straight to town. Don't stop."

"Martin, I can't leave you," I began, unhappy all over again to hear how distraught I sounded.

"Go!" he said harshly. "For once, don't think about it!"

He knew something I didn't.

"Okay," I said, trying to sound less tearful than I felt. I accepted the keys he handed me, the ones he'd taken from Karl's pocket. I ran back up the stairs, bundled and wrapped up Hayden. Then I stood by the front door, terrified of stepping out. I looked into the kitchen at Martin sitting by his friend on the floor. From somewhere, Martin dredged up the strength to give me an encouraging nod.

In retrospect, my agreeing to leave him sounds crazy; but at the time I was so seriously upset that Martin's request made some kind of sense to me. Though I was absolutely terrified, I stepped out into the snow holding the baby.

The cold hit me in the face. But no bullet. I was at the Jeep in four steps, looking through the windows. No phone. It had been taken. There were footprints, sure, but in the gray dim light and falling snow they were surprisingly hard to follow, and there were many other footprints in the parking area now.

So I began my trek through the falling snow clasping Hayden, who at least at this moment was quiet. I scanned the whiteness, looking for some sign of life out here in the bleak fields, but I saw nothing. A bone-scraping wind sprang up and scoured my face, and flakes clung to the knit cap I'd pulled over my hair. Hayden snuffled against my chest. I clutched him closer.

It was no great distance to the copse, perhaps not even

a half mile, but the ground was uneven and the contours concealed by the snow. Halfway there I became aware that I was crying, and I nuzzled the baby's cheek as if he could comfort me. I knew something was wrong with my husband, and yet he had told me to leave him. Did Martin think the shooter would come around the house to make sure of Rory, and therefore invent some reasoning to make sure I left?

And then I realized why Martin had told me to take Hayden.

Hayden was my insurance.

Martin knew the shooter wouldn't try for me if I was holding the baby. Hayden was the whole point of this. I wasn't even sure what "this" was, but Hayden was the center. Now I had the protection of Hayden's presence: and Martin didn't.

I nearly decided to turn back twice, even stopped and physically began to reverse, but I couldn't seem to figure out anything. I was shocked and freezing and desperate, and the remembered urgency of Martin's tone kept me on my course.

The snow and the baby and the rough ground made the walk seem twice as long as it actually was, but finally I was among the trees. There was Karl's black pickup, carefully parked so it was unobtrusive. I got the keys from my pocket and climbed in awkwardly, the baby making an upset choky noise in protest at the continued cold.

I laid Hayden on the floor on the passenger side. That was the best I could do. Then I scooted the seat up so my feet could reach the pedals. The pickup started on the first turn of the key just like the Jeep had, which was a real blessing, and it had an automatic shift, which was another blessing. The heater roared into life, and after a few minutes I felt a sheer, pathetic gratitude for the onset of warmth. I began backing out of the trees. When I'd turned the truck to face the road, I saw a little track at least two vehicles had made. Under those tracks must be the dirt road Margaret had told me about.

I followed them up the gentle slope to the county road, figuring the smoothest ground would lie that way, and though the pickup lurched a couple of times, we reached the road in one piece.

I started to turn the wheel left, toward town. Then I thought longingly of the Granberrys to the right, so much closer.

But Martin had said to go to town, and Martin always had a reason for making a decision. So I prepared to turn left, and I peered both ways to see if anything was coming.

It surprised me that something was.

And to compound the surprise, the traveler was Margaret Granberry, in her Dodge pickup. She stopped when she saw me by the side of the road and lowered her window.

"What are you doing?" she called. "Isn't that Karl's truck?"

"Margaret, you should get home and lock the doors!" I yelled. "Someone came up to the house and shot him!"

"Shot *Karl*?" Margaret's pale face looked even whiter, and she jumped out of her truck, which she left running in the middle of the road, and made her way swiftly over the packed snow to my window, her hands shoved in her pockets.

"He's bad," I told her. "I have to get to town to get help."

"What about Martin? And Rory?" Margaret asked.

"Rory's dead," I said baldly.

"So you left the baby there?"

Just then Hayden began crying, and I looked down to the floorboard to make sure he was okay.

When I looked back to the window, Margaret had a gun in her hand.

"Oh shit," I breathed. "Don't shoot, Margaret."

"I won't if you'll come without any trouble."

"Sure," I said instantly.

"Then you bend over and pick up my baby."

I did, though it was difficult to maneuver both our bundled bodies in the cab of the pickup.

Margaret stepped back from the door. "Now, get out holding the baby. And don't try anything like throwing him at me to get me to drop the gun."

"I wouldn't dream of that," I said indignantly, and then told myself it would be a good thing to keep my mouth shut.

Margaret's head was uncovered, and her red hair had caught a lot of snowflakes. She turned her head uneasily from side to side, like she was tracking movements invisible to me.

I slid down off the high seat, holding Hayden.

Margaret seemed to be thinking hard.

"Go get in my pickup," she ordered. "You're going to have to drive."

So I struggled uphill to the road, praying for more traffic to come along. This wasn't the day for my prayers to be answered the way I wanted them to be. The road was empty as far as I could see, north to south.

Following Margaret's directions, I got in the driver's seat, having slid Hayden over to the passenger side. The truck, still running, was older than Karl's fancy pickup, and it had seen harder usage. Before I could do more than formulate the thought that I could throw the truck in drive and take off, Margaret had grabbed Hayden and was getting in herself, the gun pointed at me.

"Go up to your driveway," she instructed.

I drove slowly, still hoping someone else would come along and read something strange into the situation, call the police. I turned in when she told me to, only to reverse and back out into the road again, this time pointed south.

"We've already turned into your driveway twice, so that ought to account for our tracks," Margaret said. "With more snow falling, it'll be hard to read the tracks anyway."

I wondered what Martin had thought when he'd heard the truck, near the house. He'd probably thought help had come quicker than he'd expected. He'd have felt proud of me...

Instead, I'd been tricked, and I hadn't gotten help.

Shame broke over me in a wave of blackness.

It was followed by a rage so overwhelming that I had trouble seeing the road ahead of me. I seldom lose my temper, and this was far beyond that, light years beyond. I knew I had blocked from my complete awareness, until this moment, just how bad Martin had looked, just how much he too needed a doctor.

Now this woman was keeping me from getting help for him, and Karl, too. I remembered Rory's empty eyes and the pool of blood around his head; but Rory was beyond human assistance, and I had no more grief for him. My sense of urgency vied with my terrible rage for supremacy in the limited emotional room I had to spare.

I tugged at my ear on my left side, away from Margaret. My earring slid out, the back rolling down my collar and into my shirt. The small earring, just a little gold knot design, went down in the deep crack of the seat. Some policeman would find it and nail Margaret Granberry, I hoped most devoutly.

Aurora Was Here.

I pressed my fingers to the wheel, the steering column, the seat adjustor, the window, as unobtrusively as possible, hoping she'd overlook a print when she wiped down the truck. Maybe I'd seen too many movies and too many episodes of *America's Most Wanted,* but I was doing the best I could for myself.

Margaret told me to turn into her driveway. It was the first time I'd seen the Granberrys' house. It was a farmhouse with extras added, in keeping with what Cindy had told me about their lifestyle. Gleaming white, with spanking green shutters and a hot tub in a sunroom to the south, it was farming deluxe.

Luke came running out the front door as we lurched to a stop, his face twisted with anxiety. There was a rifle in his hands.

"What happened?" he cried.

"Look, honey!" Margaret called, holding up the baby so he could see it.

Luke's face went slack with horror.

"What have you done, sweetheart?" he asked.

"Don't worry, she was heading to town in Karl's truck.

He was parked down at the copse," Margaret explained. "But she was taking the baby with her, and I figured this might be our last chance."

"But..."

"And sweetie, she says you hit Karl too," Margaret interrupted.

"I only fired once," he said, protesting.

"The bullet went through Rory," I told them, hardly able to choke out the words through the rage.

"He's dead," Margaret said, relief clear in her voice. "So we don't have to worry about that anymore."

Luke's shoulders slumped with the same relief. "Let's get you all inside the house," he said briskly.

"I can show Lucas his nursery," Margaret said, delight coursing through her voice.

"Hayden," I said.

"No, that's the nasty name *she* gave him," Margaret told Hayden's scrunched little face. "His real name is Lucas."

While her attention was riveted on the baby, I risked a glance at Luke. He, too, was looking at Hayden. If he hadn't been armed, I would have had him, and at the moment I felt equal to a pro boxer. Nothing would have stopped me, if I hadn't known I had to ask him for something.

"You have to call an ambulance and send it to the farm," I said, sounding as reasonable as I could, considering I was in a frenzy.

"Why? Rory's dead!"

"I realize he's beyond consideration," I said, hardly knowing what words were issuing from my mouth. "But Karl is very badly hurt and Martin is not well. I'm afraid he's...I'm afraid he's...really sick." I was making a superhuman effort to sound calm and matter-of-fact.

The couple looked at each other, communing silently.

"Don't think we can risk it," Luke said.

Margaret started into the house. "No," she threw over her shoulder, "I don't see how we can."

"You have to," I said. I stood in the snow, looking up at Luke, whose brown eyes were clear and blank. "You can't let my husband die. You can't."

"Margaret? Maybe we could send an ambulance?" he called to her, though he kept his guard on me.

"I'll bet they can trace a nine-one-one call," she said doubtfully. "Let's get inside and think about it. I bet our baby is hungry."

They weren't going to help.

That was the final straw.

I jumped him, rifle and all.

I woke up on a floor, a cold concrete floor. It was in a windowless room lit by a bulb hanging from a cord in the middle of the ceiling.

My mouth was dry as cotton and my head hurt like hell. I tried to lift it, and the effort left me shaken and nauseated. I satisfied myself with just shifting my eyes around. I thought of all the books I'd read, all the mysteries. Spenser wouldn't have ended up this way. Neither would Kinsey Milhone. Or Henry O. Or Stephanie Plum. Well, yeah, maybe Stephanie Plum.

"Hey."

I found the source of the voice. A young woman, dark

haired, was sitting on a straight-backed chair against the wall.

"Aunt Roe, are you all right?"

I hadn't realized I'd been sure Regina was dead until I saw her sitting there alive and well. But it wasn't possible for me to feel more shocked than I already did; I just accepted our niece's presence with no more than dull surprise. "Regina," I whispered.

"Yeah, it's me!" she said cheerfully. "Hey, how are you feeling? And how's the baby? I've been going nuts down here."

"Where is here?"

Regina thought that one over for a second. "Oh, you mean, where are we right now?"

"Yes," I said, without the energy to be exasperated.

"We're in the Granberrys' basement."

I'd never had a full basement. Not that many houses in Georgia do. I'd only opened the door to the basement in Martin's old farmhouse, shuddered at the dark cold that rolled up the stairs, and shut the door with alacrity. Now here I was in a basement, a windowless, below-ground prison.

"How long have you been here?"

"Since that night at your place. Well, minus the trip back to Ohio, but I don't remember much of that. Margaret gave me a bunch of sleeping pills."

I knew anguish was waiting just around the corner. When Luke Granberry had knocked me out, he'd done me a favor. I tried to stave off the misery for a few minutes. "Tell me what happened," I croaked.

"Oh, well, the Granberrys showed up," Regina said,

making a face as if Margaret and Luke were particularly undesirable party crashers.

"Why?"

"Well... you know... to get the baby. But Craig beat them there."

"Why?"

"Well... to get the baby."

I felt a tear roll down my cheek sideways on its way to the floor. Martin, alone with the dying Karl Bagosian, waiting for the ambulance I was supposed to send, the help I was supposed to bring... "Tell me from the beginning," I said, in a voice I didn't recognize as my own.

"When I got pregnant, it was like, a big disaster. You can imagine!"

No, I couldn't.

"I'd just married Craig. Well, it happened before we got married, if you can count you can figure that out, and you better believe the old ladies around here can count! Especially after my mother had that baby, you know, the big scandal."

"Yes."

"But we got married, so hey, everything was cool. But I still didn't tell anybody, because frankly, I was thinking about getting rid of it. I mean, I'm just too young to have a baby. Right?"

"Yes."

"And the idea of Craig as a daddy, well, that just didn't feel right. But I wasn't throwing up or anything, felt great, so I just decided to wait a while and see how I felt. A baby might be kind of neat. They love you, right?"

A tear flowed down my other cheek.

"So, anyway, I began showing. Craig and Rory thought that was just amazing. Feeling the baby move. But I still thought about getting rid of it. Then the Granberrys showed up one night and told us they'd been thinking."

"And?"

"Well, they said they really really wanted a baby and they couldn't have one, and they had noticed I was gonna have one, and they wondered since we were kind of strapped for money, if we would consider letting them adopt the kid? That seemed like a great idea the more we thought about it, Rory and Craig and me, so I told them, sure. They paid for me to go to the midwife, one in the next county so no one from Corinth would see me, and they asked me not to go to town, because they didn't want anyone telling the baby where he'd come from until they decided it was time. That seemed right to me, too, so I just hung out at the farm. It was boring, let me tell you!"

"I'm sure," I murmured, feeling the hair on either side of my face grow damp as the tears flowed. The basement was lined with shelves and crowded with odds and ends. I saw that Regina had made a sort of nest for herself in one corner. There was an ancient easy chair, a lamp, and a board across two cement blocks that served as a table beside the chair. It was piled high with magazines. A mattress topped with a sleeping bag was pushed against the wall. There was a cubicle that I suspected hid a toilet and maybe a shower, close to the base of the stairs.

"Have you tried to escape yet?" I asked, interrupting Regina's account of the onset of her labor. She sounded exactly like she was the only woman in the world who'd ever had a baby.

Regina gaped at me. "Are you kidding?" she asked incredulously. "As soon as Craig and Rory show up with the baby, Margaret'll let me go. I'm just, like, a hostage! If I tried to escape, they might hurt me!"

Ah-oh. She didn't know. If I could have felt worse, I would have. "What do you think happened in Lawrenceton?"

"See, I had the baby," Regina said, and I sighed. She was not going to edit her adventures. "And when I saw him, I just thought I couldn't give him up. And Craig got put in jail, so he couldn't make me. I told Margaret and Luke I had to breastfeed for the first few days, that the midwife had told me so, but really I'd had the shot to dry my boobs up. I just said that so I could take him home with me. But I knew the Granberrys were dying for me to give him up; they'd been pestering me from the hour I had him."

"So you ran?"

"Yeah, man, I just took off. I didn't think that Craig and Rory would figure out where I'd gone. And I never thought they'd get out so quick. I mean, I missed them, Craig especially. But I couldn't make up my mind. And I had really thought the Granberrys would be great for the baby, but then I began thinking Margaret was a little weird, and she could make Luke do anything. So maybe she wouldn't be a good mother. And," Regina's voice lost its bounce, "I really loved the baby. I kind of wanted to keep him, even if we really needed the money. So one day when I knew the Granberrys had gone into the city for some art thing, I lit out."

"The Granberrys had already paid you some?"

"Oh, yeah, they gave us half the cash when he was born. They were gonna give us the other half when we turned him over. I hid the money, except for some I took out for the trip."

She'd hidden it in the crib mattress. Where Rory had found it.

"What about the legal part of it?"

"Margaret said she and Luke'd move as soon as the baby was old enough. She figured wherever she lived, no one would ask questions. She read a couple of books on how to get a birth certificate for him. You know you can get books that tell you how to do that? She was gonna change his name to Lucas. I just called him Hayden for my great-uncle on my father's side. He was my favorite when I was a little girl."

I thought about all this. Finally, I told Regina I was thirsty, and she jumped up to bring me some water in a plastic cup. There was a sink on the wall, stained and ugly and old, but functional. Regina slid a hand under my head so I could raise it enough to sip from the cup.

"What's wrong with my head?" I asked, staving off the inevitable. Besides, I did want to know.

"I guess Luke hit you with the stock of his rifle. Margaret says you jumped him! That was kind of crazy, Aunt Roe."

"Yes," I agreed.

"Anyway, you have this big bruise and swollen place on your forehead, it goes up into your hair, and a little blood dried on your face. So, have you seen Craig? When's he coming to get me? Did Rory get sick in Lawrenceton? He sure was acting awful funny."

"What do you remember about that night?" Hard to believe it had only been five days.

Regina looked down at me doubtfully. She was sitting on the floor beside me now, the cup still in her hand. I became aware I was lying on yet another sleeping bag, and she was crouched on the cold concrete. Her black hair was a mass of tangles and her eyes were puffy.

"After you guys left to go to that dinner, I was in your house fixing up some supper, one of those Healthy Choice microwave meals you had in the freezer."

I would have nodded if my neck wouldnt've snapped.

"Then I heard a car pull up, and I knew it wasn't you because you guys were gonna be gone longer. So I look out, and it was a black kid. He was real polite, said a friend had brought him out to get his dad's truck. I thought I saw something fall out of the back of the trailer as he was turning it around, but I didn't tell him. I figured I'd go pick it up later. After he'd driven the truck out of your backyard, and the guy who'd given him a ride had followed him out of the driveway, Craig and Rory turned in. They came into the house with me, and we started fighting almost right away. I was mad. I'd left because I needed time to think, and here he was right on my tail.

"I began to get a little nervous, alone with the guys, them being so mad at me. Course Craig would never hurt me, but he was really furious, it was the worst fight we'd ever had." Regina's face softened. "He's usually so sweet," she said almost tenderly. "It was one reason I almost kept the baby."

I had my serious doubts that Craig had been the baby's father. In my secret brain compartment where I keep a lot of thoughts I want to hide from myself, I'd stored the idea that the baby looked much more like Rory. Rory's baby picture, framed in his sister's house, had been the spitting image of Hayden. "So Rory began feeling bad?" I asked weakly.

"Yeah, he was acting really strange. He said he was so sleepy he couldn't stand up, and I told him to go lie on the couch. He said some blond-haired woman, some older gal in a fancy car, had asked them to help her in the liquor store parking lot, and she gave them a couple of beers to say thank you, I think her car had gotten stuck in a dip or something, and they'd helped her rock it out. Rory thought there'd been something in the beer; he said when he got through there were some speckles in the bottom of the bottle."

"So you went over to the garage apartment?"

"Yeah, actually, Craig and I..." And here Regina turned coy. In between quarrels, they'd wanted a passionate reunion, apparently.

"You took Hayden?"

"Yeah, sure, we couldn't leave him in the house over there, with Rory out of it! On the way over, Craig picked up something from the yard. It was a hatchet, from the back of the guy's pickup, and he put it on the steps so the guy would see it if he missed it and came back."

That was where the hatchet had come from. One small question explained.

"So you took the baby over to the apartment."

Regina turned a dull, unbecoming red. "He was asleep," she said defensively. "We didn't have time to put up that crib thing, so I laid him in his infant seat in the recline position."

"Then?"

"Well, before things got... serious, you know... we heard *another* car pull up, and Craig said, 'Hey, what is this place, Grand Central Station?' and I looked out the front window and it was the Granberrys!" Regina shook her head. "I said, 'Craig, you're not gonna believe this!' and he says, 'Hey, we're not letting them have our baby, cause here they are following us!' and I said, 'You're right, let's keep Hayden.'" Regina sighed, offered me some more water.

I started to shake my head no, then realized that was a very bad idea. "No," I said. "Thanks." I wondered if Regina had ever made a reasoned decision in her life.

"While Craig was zipping up, getting ready to go down the stairs, I took the baby and kind of slid him under the bed. He was so sound asleep, he didn't even peep. He's so good! I didn't want them to walk in and see him and get all grabby, like they did once before. I told Craig what to say."

"Why didn't the Granberrys get there when Craig and Rory did?"

"Well, they'd stopped to eat. At the last gas station they'd stopped at, Craig and Rory had asked for directions to Lawrenceton, so Margaret and Luke knew where they were going. When they were talking later about following Craig, they said they'd been scared to follow too close. When they got to Lawrenceton, they just looked in the phone book for familiar names, came up with Bartell in five minutes."

"So, what happened then?" I closed my eyes, listened to Regina's voice wash over me. She was glad to have someone to talk to, so glad she hadn't noticed I hadn't answered any of her questions.

"I heard Craig yelling at them, telling them he'd decided they couldn't have his boy after all. That he'd been willing because a deal was a deal, but now they'd tracked him down from Ohio and he didn't like that at all. So after a while, Margaret came in the room, she said Luke was down there talking to Craig, where was the baby?"

"And you told her—?"

"The same thing I'd told Craig to tell Luke. That you and Martin had the baby, that you'd taken him riding with you so he would go to sleep, that you wouldn't be coming back for a long time."

"She want to know where Rory was?"

"I told her he was over in the house."

"So?"

"So, she wrote him a long note and stuck it under the windshield wiper of their car. I don't know what it said, not everything, cause she had pulled a gun on me by that time. You could have knocked me over with a feather, Margaret Granberry pulling a gun on me! So I was sitting there, quiet, and I couldn't fight, because Hayden was there under the bed and who knew what would happen to him? And I was scared to death he'd wake up and make a noise."

"But he didn't."

"She looked around the room, but she never thought of looking under the bed," Regina said. "So she told me to get in my car, we were going to drive some."

"And you went down the stairs?"

"Yes. It was hard to leave Hayden, but I knew once we left, Craig and Rory would search for him; Craig knew for sure he was in that room!" Regina beamed fondly.

"Where was Craig when you left?"

"Oh, he and Luke were still arguing. Craig didn't say anything when he saw me coming out without the baby, and I knew he'd take care of Hayden and come after me."

I took a deep breath, and my head throbbed as though it were splitting.

"Aunt Roe," she said suddenly, "what are you and Uncle

Martin doing in Corinth? Every now and then if Margaret and Luke are talking in this room right overhead I can hear them through the gap around the dryer vent, and I heard that you were at the farm. Doesn't anyone know where I am? Aren't Craig and Rory looking for me? Why do you have Hayden?"

I had to tell her about us bringing the baby and Rory back to Corinth, about what had happened before we'd brought them here. It wasn't kind to let her ignorance go on any longer, though I still had lots of questions.

"So when you and Margaret drove off in your car," I began, "Luke was still arguing outside with Craig?"

"Yeah, they were standing on the steps."

Where Craig had left the hatchet. While the note to Rory began to disintegrate in the rain. What had Regina imagined the note said? Why hadn't Regina figured the Granberrys had no reason to leave Rory a note if they planned to leave Craig there alive?

"Regina," I said, trying to sound gentle, succeeding only in sounding weary, "after you left, Luke killed Craig."

Regina stared down at me. "Why would he do that?" she asked finally. Her voice had a tremor in it.

"I guess they fought," I said. "Craig didn't want Luke to have Hayden. You both had gone back on your agreement. Luke was mad." Regina didn't seem to have much grasp of consequences.

"What about Rory? Did Luke go in the house and kill him too?"

"No. Luke needed him to stay, get the baby back, and return him to Corinth. I suppose in the note… Margaret promised him more money if he brought the baby to them.

But we brought the baby, and we wouldn't have given him up to Rory. All Rory was, was a problem. So today, Luke shot Rory."

I could see the whites all around Regina's irises.

"Both gone," she whispered. "Then why am I alive?"

That was a good question, and unexpectedly astute of Regina if she'd meant it literally. While she sat in disbelieving silence, I gave her the bare bones of our trip to Corinth, of what had happened at the farm this afternoon.

And I had to tell her that Margaret and Luke had the baby.

Regina began to cry, but I had no comfort to offer her. My own problems overwhelmed me. I couldn't move without waves of pain and nausea, and I could no longer put off my fear for Martin. I didn't have enough energy to worry about Karl Bagosian, too; I thought, obscurely, He's got plenty of family, and I did my best to dismiss him from my mind.

My thoughts wandered away from the chilly cellar and the stupid young woman beside me. I fantasized that maybe Martin had managed to make it to the road and was flagging down some passing car. That was the least taxing way to get help I could imagine. Even then, the struggle down the snowy driveway, the long cold wait... I remembered how sick Martin had looked, and I wondered what was wrong.

After a while, I admitted to myself that I figured it was his heart.

I recalled Martin's hesitance when I asked him about his physical, in what seemed the long-ago past. I suspected that Martin had learned then that something was going wrong inside him. But with the troubles of his family, and the troubles of my family, he'd thought it best to put off having that explored; that was what I would have done, and I was sure Martin would think that way.

"You think Uncle Martin will get us out?" Regina asked, in a voice worn limp with tears.

I lay there and hated her. "He didn't look good when I last saw him," I said. "Over at the farmhouse."

"We're on our own?" Regina sounded as if that were unbelievable. All her layers of backup, gone. I could sympathize. "Have you heard from my mother?"

"Not a word."

"So she's still on her cruise," Regina said. She sat for a long time in silence, which I welcomed. When she finally spoke, it was hardly reassuring. "So they'll kill us, now that they've got the baby," she said, and I whispered, "Yes." She'd reasoned herself to the end of the line.

We fell silent. We waited.

11

Later, I thought of asking Regina if the Granberrys kept any dogs.

"No," she said, obviously thinking I was an utter loon.

"Good." Any idea of escape would be complicated by dogs.

Once we heard Hayden crying upstairs, and both of us twitched as if we were going to rise and tend to him. (In my case, that meant my arm moved.) I knew that sooner or later I was going to have to get up and go to the bathroom, and I dreaded it . . . when I had any dread to spare.

Margaret and Luke didn't put in an appearance. Probably totally wrapped up with their new baby, I thought bitterly. Though I wanted them both to die in agony, if they were going to live I wanted them to bring me some Extra-Strength Tylenol.

I slept some, though it wasn't like normal sleep; it was suspiciously like falling unconscious. Regina moaned and wept. I couldn't blame her, but the noise grated at the terrible sore ache in my head. Finally my bladder couldn't hold out any longer, and I talked my niece into helping me up.

The trip to the little room at the foot of the stairs was

about as much fun as I thought it'd be. At least I emptied myself completely in one trip, since I threw up. I knew I had a concussion, but people survived concussions—right? In mystery novels, the hero always checked out of the hospital when he had a concussion, and went on about solving the case. I knew what books I would throw across the room in the future, providing I had a future.

Also, detectives in books seemed to take as many aspirin as they wanted, without regard for the recommended adult dosage. Was I the only person in the world who watched the clock so I wouldn't take my pills too close together? Though at the moment, I would take anything anyone handed me. Please, knock me out.

You can see the quality of my thinking was not high. And those were only the good parts.

I tried to concern myself about escaping. I tried to pretend I was well, and resourceful, and determined. The truth was, I was sick in body and heart, and desperate.

There was an outside door to the basement, the kind I'd only seen in movies before now; almost flat to the ground, barred on the outside. No windows. Regina assured me she'd tried that door many times, and it was of course always barred. There was nothing like a saw in the basement; the Granberrys had removed the tools. What they'd left was extra stores of canned goods, luggage, and a pile of odds and ends of lumber.

One of them would have to bring us food eventually. And after some hours, Luke did. But Margaret stood above him on the stairs, her gun in her hand.

"How's Hayden?" Regina asked, beginning to sob yet again.

"Our baby's fine," Luke said, briefly and pointedly.

I prayed Regina wouldn't ask them what they were going to do with us.

"What are you gonna do with me?" she asked. So I was only half disappointed.

Luke didn't answer, which was just as well. He set down a tray on Regina's makeshift table, and left. Margaret was vigilant the whole time. I looked as ill as possible, which was no stretch.

There was a bottle of Excedrin on the tray. Regina opened it for me, and though I was afraid it would make me sick again, I took four. What a rebel. I propped myself up on one elbow to try the soup, which was Campbell's chicken noodle, and I managed a couple of crackers and some water. I was exhausted when I lay back down.

But after about thirty minutes, I found I felt better.

"Help me up," I told Regina.

"Need to go the girls' room?"

"No, I need to move a little."

Regina had carried the tray up to the top step, which she said was normal routine. Margaret had opened the door, bent down, and removed it. It had looked to me like she was alone.

Now, after my cell mate had helped me stand, I managed to walk by myself, though "walking" makes it sound more organized than it really was. I went over to the cellar storm doors. I had to push against them for myself. They gave only a fraction of an inch. There was a dead bolt inside the cellar, of course, but at some point Regina had unbolted it and left it that way.

"What's the bar outside made of?" I asked.

"Metal," she answered gloomily. She had experimented more than she was letting on. "I did think of breaking one of the jars, putting a straight piece of glass through the gap, and sawing at the bar, if it was wood. But it wasn't."

"You were talking before like you were content just to wait down here."

"I was trying to act like I thought everything would be okay." Now that, I understood. "And I guess I figured they were more likely to let me out if they saw me assuming they were going to let me out." She shrugged. "It couldn't hurt." Her head tensed. "Listen! There's someone here!"

After a second, I could hear it, too. The front door slammed, and there were more footsteps above us. Suddenly the basement door swung open a crack.

"If you say one word I'll kill this baby," Margaret said. "Don't scream, don't say anything."

After she shut the door Regina and I stood looking at each other.

"She wouldn't hurt Hayden," I said. "Look at what she's done for him already!"

"I know . . . but . . ."

Suddenly deciding, I managed to get to the stairs, grabbed the wooden railing, began to haul myself up. Then I felt a hand gripping my pants leg.

"She might mean it," Regina said.

"Martin may already be dead," I told her. "I have to get out of here and get help for him." I was pleading.

"I'm sorry, Aunt Roe. Not if there's a chance she might hurt my baby."

And Regina, bigger and stronger, clapped a hand over my mouth, held on to me, and would not let me go. I was hardly in any shape to offer much resistance.

We could hear voices right outside the door. Several male voices, one female. Margaret.

"Come over this way where we can hear," Regina whispered, and dragged me off the stairs and over to a spot by the wall where the dryer vent fed into the basement.

I was adding my niece to the list of people I wanted to die. But for now that would have to wait, and I listened as she bid me.

"...his truck by the road," a male voice was saying. "His wife has been out looking for him."

"Is he going to be all right?" Margaret asked, and I swear there was genuine concern in her voice.

"Well, he's lost a lot of blood," the man said doubtfully. "We'll just have to wait and see. One dead, two in bad shape. They can't tell us what happened. You didn't hear any shots?"

"...heard what might have been one, late this afternoon," Luke said. His voice was much fainter.

"And you had already been down there? Everything was okay?"

"Oh, yes, fine!" Margaret. "But—I hate to say this—Martin's first wife and her boyfriend were there, and there was some bad feeling in the air."

"Dennis and Martin never did get along," the male voice said thoughtfully.

"And I really don't like to say this," Margaret said, "but it seemed to me like Dennis was kind of making eyes at Martin's new wife."

"...we don't know where she has..." the voice faded away.

If it wasn't for the baby, Regina would let me go.

If it wasn't for the baby, I would scream my head off.

If it wasn't for the baby, none of this would have happened.

No, no. If it wasn't for Regina...

No, even that was wrong. If it wasn't for the Granberrys and their desire to have what nature couldn't give them...

No, it was all of these things.

It was quiet upstairs. Our rescue had walked out the door.

Regina let me go.

I sank down on my sleeping bag, exhausted.

"I'm sorry," Regina said, when she saw my face.

I started to tell her I would never forgive her, but I think she already knew that. At least I was certain that Martin had gotten help, though I had no idea what shape he was in. "Tomorrow morning by surprise," I said, "we take them." I outlined my plan, which was based on far too little data.

"I thought you were a nice lady," Regina said, awed.

"Not anymore," I told her.

In the morning, about eight o'clock, Luke brought our tray down, Margaret covering him as she had the night before. They looked glassy-eyed, and I hoped Hayden had kept them up all night. There were two cups of orange juice and two Toaster Strudels. No coffee. Well, good. That would make me meaner, having to go without my coffee.

We ate. I took more Excedrin. I felt about like you'd expect—hell warmed over—but at least I'd slept fitfully. After we'd used the bathroom and washed our faces in the sink, Regina carried the tray up the stairs and put it on the small landing right inside the door as she had the night before.

She came down and stood before me. "You're sure you can do this?" she asked me. I could tell by the look on her face that I looked bad.

"I'm a lot more worried about you than me," I said, with mistimed bluntness. "Do you want your baby back?"

"Yes," she said fiercely. "The people that killed his dad can't raise him."

Discovering she was a widow had tempered Regina overnight. I looked in her eyes and saw only determination. It almost matched the desperation I felt, the absolute necessity of reaching my husband to find out what had happened to him. Only that desperation got me up off the sleeping bag, pushed me up the stairs.

I stood, one foot on the landing just inside the door and one foot on the next step down, with my back to the wall, looking over the wooden handrail at the open space of the basement, reviewing what I had to do. I glanced at my watch; it was nine o'clock.

Then there was only the waiting. If it were the much larger Luke instead of Margaret, if for once it were both of them retrieving the tray… then we were sunk. I was counting entirely on them being accustomed to Regina's passivity.

I had been hearing someone moving around in the

room right outside the door, which Regina had told me was the kitchen. Now the footsteps became clearer.

The lock clicked, the door began to open, and I took a deep breath. A head appeared as the door swung open and touched the wall right by my hand.

Margaret had come alone for the tray.

She'd bent to pick it up before she noticed me flattened against the wall. And by then I'd reached up, grabbed that long red hair, and yanked with all my might.

Adrenaline had come to my aid, and since I pulled myself back sharply, Margaret shot past me at a good clip, unable even to get a sound out, which was great. She was hurt by the fall, but I don't know how badly, because when she reached the bottom of the steps, Regina lifted a board that had been part of the pile of lumber, and hit Margaret Granberry's head with all her might.

There was a slight crunching noise, and Margaret lay silent at the foot of the stairs.

"Ick," said Regina, panting.

My thoughts exactly.

Regina came up the stairs behind me, having stepped over Margaret quite casually.

I picked up the tray to get it out of our way, and took a cautious step into the kitchen. Margaret had propped the rifle by the door, I noticed. Fat lot of good that had done her.

The kitchen was a beautiful sunny room floored with white linoleum. The sun was bouncing off the snow outside and into the room through gleaming windows. My eyes were dazzled by the brightness.

On my right there was an open door into a den or

living room, to my left a closed door that I thought led to the outside. I'd have been in more of a mood to appreciate Margaret's decorating skills if Luke Granberry hadn't stomped in the back door just then with an armful of wood.

His face was almost funny when he saw me, and the fact that I had the tray in my hands, as he'd expected Margaret to have, seemed to compound his confusion. I threw the tray at him, and the kitchen was clean no longer.

He dropped his armful of logs and orange juice splattered his pants. He stared down at them in bewilderment.

And suddenly, as if I'd walked into a wall, I ran out of strength. I sank to my knees, and was hard put to it not to fall on my side. The pain in my head throbbed and pulsed, and my legs felt like Jell-O.

Luke looked up from his assessment of the stain to say, "Regina, don't do that." His eyes were fixed on a spot behind me and a little to his left.

"You killed my husband," Regina said. "You took my baby. Now you go get him and hand him to Aunt Roe."

I managed to turn my head enough to see that Regina was holding the rifle. I wondered if she knew how to fire it.

Luke didn't move. "You don't understand, Regina. Where's Margaret?" he asked, and I saw the beginning of panic on his face.

"I think I'll just go get Hayden myself," Regina said, and shot Luke.

I sat on the floor, paralyzed and gaping. When Regina changed, she didn't mess around. She went full circle.

In the next second, I was aware that I was alone in the kitchen with the moaning Luke Granberry. He was curled in a ball just inside the still-open door. Cold air was pouring in and he was clutching his right shoulder. His coat was stained with blood.

I pulled myself up until I stood with my hands on the kitchen table. I wondered where the car keys were. Then I spied the telephone. I staggered over to it, took it off the wall. I was so sure it would be dead, it was an almost painful shock to find it worked perfectly.

Margaret had neatly posted emergency numbers on the wall beside the phone. I punched in the sheriff's number.

"Come get me," I said to the man who answered. "I've been hurt and I'm too weak to drive and I have to get to the hospital."

"What's your location, ma'am?"

I hadn't the slightest idea.

"I'm at the Granberry farm," I said.

"What's that route number?"

I remembered. "Eight. It's right next to the old Bartell farm," I said.

"Oh, all right, south of town, that would be."

"Please hurry."

"What's the nature of your emergency?"

"Oh, shit! Just come! There are dead people out here!" I said, and hung up. Stupid man. That would bring them, though the Granberrys might not be dead. Hurt bad, surely that would qualify.

"Here's Hayden," Regina said, her voice almost a coo.

I scarcely looked at him. If I'd said, "So?" Regina

might've shot me. All my energy was bent on lasting, staying upright, until I could see Martin again. "He looks fine," I said. My voice came out more like a whisper. I was feeling more like my old self every minute, Aurora Teagarden the librarian, whereas Regina seemed permanently transformed into Iron Woman.

But maybe I would never be my old self, I reflected after a moment, since I seemed to be able to ignore Luke's moaning.

I thought of getting the keys and driving Margaret's pickup or Luke's Bronco into town, to save time, but then I had to admit to myself that I would probably pass out along the way. I sank into a chair and put my head on my arms. Regina sat next to me, holding her son, and together we waited for the sirens to get closer.

They even searched Hayden, to make sure he wasn't packing heat in his diaper, I guess.

"Take me to my husband," I said, and I said it to every officer who came in the door.

It pleased me that they believed us pretty quickly, after they'd been down in the basement and seen the evidence of our imprisonment. But believing isn't the same as releasing, and it was all too long before the sheriff himself decided to drive me to the little hospital in Corinth.

"They're going to transfer Mr. Bartell to Pittsburgh when he's stable enough," the sheriff told me.

"He had a heart attack?" I asked.

"Yes," the sheriff confirmed, his wide Slavic face looking so sorry for me that my heart sank.

I made myself ask about Karl.

"He's in critical condition, but he lasted this long," Sheriff Brod told me. "Karl Bagosian is a tough bird. He hasn't been able to tell us exactly what happened. Would you like to tell me?"

"My husband and Karl were standing in the kitchen with my niece's friend, Rory," I said wearily, staring out the squad car window at the frozen fields. To me, it was an alien landscape. The cold sun made it gleam like the white linoleum in the Granberrys' kitchen. I saw the blood against it, heard Luke moaning again like an animal.

I got through the account of what had happened, yet again.

I could tell the sheriff had a hard time believing I'd started Margaret down the stairs. I was a librarian, for God's sake. I reached up and touched the dreadful bruise and swelling on my forehead. I'd gotten a good look in the Granberrys' bathroom mirror. Even touching as delicately as possible, my head rang with pain.

"You need to get checked out at the hospital," the sheriff said. He was a big man, wide faced and heavy.

"After I see Martin," I said, and didn't speak again until we were there.

"I just want you to know, ma'am, that the deputy that questioned the Granberrys last night… well, he won't go without an official reprimand."

I shrugged. It didn't matter anymore.

Somehow I was in a wheelchair going down corridors freshly painted in a glossy beige. The rubberized flooring was a dark chocolate brown. The place smelled like a sure-enough hospital, the sharp odors of disinfectants and medicine and the bland smell of hospital food vying for supremacy.

Through the doors marked ICU we went, the nurse pushing me not offering any comment no matter how many questions I asked her. The tiny ICU unit had room for six patients, and Martin and Karl were the only two.

Cindy was in Martin's glass-sided room, and she stepped out when she saw me coming. She started to say something to me and then thought better of it. Her eyes were red.

The nurse wheeled me right up to Martin's bed. I looked at him in horror. His face had lost all its normal color, and everything that could be hooked up to a tube was. He looked twenty years older.

"He hasn't said much," the young man in the shadows of the room told me, and I saw that it was Barrett.

I knew then that Martin was going to die.

"Sweetheart," I said, trying to keep my voice from shaking. "I'm here." I stood and took his hand.

His eyes flickered open. He took in the bruise. "You got hurt," he said faintly. "That's why you didn't come."

"Yes."

"I knew it."

"Miss me?" I said, trying to smile, having no idea what to say.

"Oh, yes," he breathed, almost smiling.

"I missed you, too," I said, choking on the words.

My eyes brimmed and welled over. I kissed him on his cheek, and wished with all my heart I was alone with him. But I couldn't tell his son to leave.

That meant Barrett was there when Martin gave a

rattling breath five minutes later and alarms went off, and Barrett was there when the technicians hustled us out in the hall and worked over my husband, and Barrett was there when the old doctor came out minutes later to tell me that my husband had died.

I became a widow the same week as Regina, the same week Luke Granberry became a widower.

Regina had been deprived of both of the men she'd cared for; I'm not going to assume she loved them. Her mother had returned and promised to help her raise the baby, whom Barby claimed was the spitting image of a Bartell. I never held Hayden in my arms again. Somehow I never wanted to.

Regina faced only nominal charges in the death of Margaret Granberry, since Luke himself attested they had held Regina and me prisoner. Without Margaret, Luke seemed to lose all his resolve, to become indifferent to his own life. But he recovered from his bullet wound to face three charges of kidnapping (Regina, Hayden, and me), two counts of murder (Craig and Rory), one count of assault with a deadly weapon (Karl). Since Luke pled guilty, I didn't have to return to Corinth for the trial.

I would never go there again.

Two weeks after Craig's funeral, Craig's older brother, Dylan, charged Regina with being an unfit mother, citing her plan to sell her baby to the Granberrys. He and his wife, Shondra, wanted to raise Hayden along with their little girl.

But Regina and Barby together had too much Bartell determination for the judge. He ruled the baby should stay with his mother, but the judge did order Regina to take parenting classes.

She met an older man at the first session, a divorced thirty-year-old ordered to take the class after he'd slapped his child in a grocery store, and the next thing I knew, they were married. Regina seemed to slip into marriage easily, not seeing it as so different from any other state of being.

Of course that was months after I had brought Martin back to Lawrenceton for the funeral. Cindy had hinted that there was room in Martin's parents' plot, and Barby had done more than hint. But I can be mighty deaf when I feel like it. It was none of Cindy's business; ex was ex. And Barby had never been a favorite of mine.

Poor Mother. She had to try to tone down her joy at her husband John's complete recovery from his heart attack, and he was twenty years older than Martin. I saw her efforts and pitied her in a remote way.

Poor John stood by the graveside trying not to look guilty. John was a rock to me, and his children, too. I'd always resented them a little, maybe, having been the sole child of my mother until she remarried, but his two sons and their wives were so kind and tactful that my petty irritation seeped away.

I was still in the stunned shell of numbness when the letter came. I'd stopped at the mailbox on my way back from work, and I shuffled through its contents indifferently. Bills, catalogs, occupant mail. But there was one personal letter, hand-written, no return address.

I slit it open when I got into the house.

I glanced at the signature. It was from Luke Granberry.

I dropped it as if it were a loathsome spider. But seconds later, I picked it back up.

Dear Mrs. Bartell,

I know you will never forgive me for what I have done but I wanted you to know why I even thought of it.

Margaret and I moved to Corinth because I had discovered my mother lived there. At least for a while.

I think Margaret told you I was adopted. I was lucky to be adopted by wonderful people. Not only loving, but rich. My dad had made a lot of money in the tire business.

Like most adopted children, I always wondered who my real mother and father were. I didn't want to ask my mom and dad. I knew it would upset them. But I always felt that they knew my mother's name, that they had met her at the unwed mothers' home, from something Dad let fall once. After I married Margaret, she became as determined as I was to find out, and she was a lot smarter than me at thinking of ways to do it. When my mother died, Margaret went through all her papers, thinking she might find some trace, and sure enough she found a private detective's report on a Barbara Bartell Lampton. My mom had kept track of my birth mother that way. Why, I don't know. I guess she wanted to know how Barbara turned out. When Margaret read the old story about Barby, the story about my mother getting thrown out of her stepfather's church because of an illegitimate pregnancy, Margaret knew she'd found my birth mother.

From the reports, we found out that Barbara didn't live in Corinth anymore, but my sister Regina did. So we bought the farm next to the one where Regina was living and set out to make friends with her. We'd always wanted a baby, and when we saw what a mess Regina was likely to make of her pregnancy, we felt like we had to take a hand. It seemed just exactly right since Margaret and I had tried so hard for so long. If we couldn't have one of our own, one that was partly ours by blood was next best. Margaret never got over that woman in our building thinking we would like to have her baby. She said she told you that story, about the woman leaving her baby at our door.

We did everything for Regina without telling her I was her brother. We made her go for her checkups. We paid for some of her groceries, so she'd eat the right food. We even went through Lamaze, hoping she'd let us be there at the birth, but she didn't want us there. She'd rather have those two thugs there. At least she was sure one of them was the father of the child.

We just wanted the baby. We couldn't kill Regina when it would have been so easy to. No one would have known. But she is my sister, and I just couldn't. We believed her that night when she told us you and your husband had the baby. Margaret never could have imagined that Regina would leave her baby, even for a moment, under a bed.

What I want to let you know is, we never planned for any of this to happen when we first found out who my mother is. I wanted to know that, and I wanted a child of my own and Margaret's. I had a right to those things. I still think so. If Craig and Rory had just stayed out of it, and I had been able to deal with Regina on my own, it would have worked out, since she's my sister.

I'm sorry.

Luke Granberry

I looked at this letter for a long time after I read it. I wondered if Regina and Barby needed to know about Luke. I decided that wasn't my responsibility.

I went outside into the cold dry air with a match from the box on the mantelpiece. I hadn't had the spirit to build a fire all winter, from the wood Darius Quattermain had strewn around the yard, the wood that Martin and I had gathered up and stacked . . . I headed my thoughts off before I could tear up. I struck the match against a brick, and it ignited beautifully. I set the letter on fire and, when I could no longer hold it, I dropped it into an empty flowerpot I'd never put away in the toolshed.

I thought about Darius again, though, about his singing and dancing in the chilly wind. I thought about the drug he'd been slipped, and about Rory's unexpected sleeping jag after the woman at the liquor store had bought them beers in exchange for their help in getting her car out of a trough.

I grabbed my keys and drove back into town. Mostly these days I just drove to work and back, and the spontaneous errand felt very odd.

I knocked on the Lowrys' door ten minutes later. As I'd hoped, Catledge hadn't gotten home yet. Ellen was by herself.

"Come in," she said instantly, all graciousness. "How've you been doing?" Everyone said that now. As if I'd tell them.

I stepped in, sure I was about to ruin my welcome for good, not caring. "You were the one doing it," I said without preamble. "You put the pills in Mr. Quattermain's bottle, and you drugged the beer you gave Rory Brown."

"Rory Brown?" Ellen's smooth brow wrinkled in

puzzlement. "Oh, was he the scruffy blond boy at the liquor store?"

"Yes. He described you to me, and I remembered you coming in the garage door with that bottle of wine. You weren't acting like yourself."

"That's funny," Ellen said coolly. "I thought I was acting very much like myself."

"Are you that cruel?"

"For a time, I was."

I stared at her with something like hatred. Who knew how things would have turned out if Rory hadn't been drugged?

"You're pathetic," I said. It was the worst thing I could think of to say.

"Yes, I am. I found all those pills in my son's room this summer. I confiscated them. Of course, I should have flushed them down the toilet, but for some reason I didn't. Catledge and I checked Tally into a drug rehabilitation program. You are the only person in this town who knows where he really is."

I took a deep breath, let it out. Some of the rage seeped out with it.

"I couldn't tell anyone. I couldn't talk to Catledge about it, he absolutely refused. The program Tally was in, the head therapist said it was important he not get any visitors for a while so he could concentrate on the agenda. Catledge didn't want me to work." She threw her hands up in the air. See how the world had frustrated her?

"Don't give me that," I said. My tone wasn't pleasant. "You could have worked anyway, no matter what Catledge said. You could have flown to wherever your son is and told them you were paying for his stay and by God you wanted to see him. You could have taken space heaters to poor old people. Instead, you slipped drugs to the unwary."

Ellen looked down at me coldly. "I won't do it again," she said. "For one thing, I'm out of pills. But I've got to say, I kind of enjoyed it." She gestured toward the door and I left.

Driving home tired me out. So many things seemed to tire me these days. I spent a lot of time watching television in bed, which had involved buying another television, getting it installed in a special stand up in our bedroom, and paying a higher cable bill. Reading didn't seem as interesting to me . . . Nothing did.

Again, I pulled in the driveway and got out, looking around me at the familiar landscape.

The wind had picked up again and, as I watched, it snatched up the ashes of Luke Granberry's letter and began to scatter them from the flowerpot. I looked at the weather vane Martin had installed on the garage roof and saw that the wind was blowing the ashes west. Toward the cemetery.

ABOUT THE AUTHOR

Charlaine Harris is a *New York Times* bestselling author who has been writing for over thirty years. She was born and raised in the Mississippi River Delta area. Her Sookie Stackhouse books have appeared in twenty-five different languages and and were the basis for the HBO series *True Blood.* The Aurora Teagarden mystery series and the Midnight, Texas trilogy have also recently been adapted for television. Her latest novel, *An Easy Death*, is the first in a new series.

Also available from Charlaine Harris as a JABberwocky eBook or paperback

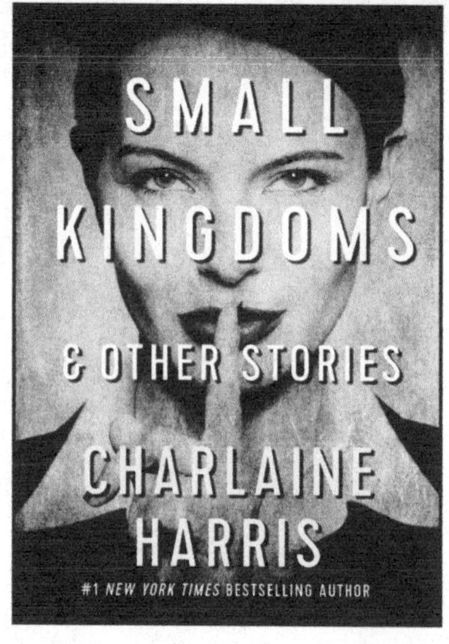